Between You, Me and the Banana Tree

By Shem Douglas

To my parents from the little island in the sun.

(Even though you never bought me a pet monkey when I was seven)

Chapter One

I had never tasted blood before. The thought of it repulsed me. But that Sunday evening it suddenly became one of my recommended five a day. I could feel it gathering speed over my top lip, and instinctively my tongue reached out to catch the first drop. I was surprised that it was warm and had a sharp metallic flavour that reminded me of sticking my tongue on those oblong-shaped batteries. I used the sleeve of my off-white T-shirt to wipe away the blood and painfully breathed in. I then steadied myself to a seated position and slowly brushed my fingers back and forth over the carpet. I hadn't noticed how coarse it had become over the years, but then I had never been this close to the ground to care.

The face of my watch was cracked. It wasn't fancy or expensive; I preferred the garish plastic watches that came from a pound shop rather than a jeweller who eyeballed you as if you were moments away from a smash-and-grab robbery. It was the crack on my neon-green watch that infuriated me the most, not the bloodied nose or the fact that he had just launched me across the landing. It was my broken wristwatch. He had broken it. Who the hell did he think he was?

I shot upright, planted my bare feet firmly into the carpet and threw myself towards their bedroom door. I had a new sense of purpose and a watch that needed to be avenged. He had bolted the door from the inside, and my banging was futile. I could hear my mother screaming from the other side of the door. If he had the audacity to throw his own daughter to the ground, what was he capable of doing to his wife, my mother?

I just wasn't strong enough. I wanted to lift the door off its hinges like a 1970s Blaxploitation heroine—Foxy Brown looking effortlessly stylish and competent with her voluminous coiffure, kicking ass and taking names. I would simply pick up the door, spin it above my head a few times and beat him with it until he begged for mercy. But all I could manage was a whimper as I punched the locked bedroom door for the last time. I recoiled in pain as the skin of my knuckles reddened and then bled.

I had seen him punch my mother before. One time with such force that her bottom lip had exploded into a flash of brilliant red against her pale white skin, spraying bright splashes of cherry that landed on the side of the kettle. Up until that moment he had only goaded me, restrained me or simply batted me out of the way like an annoying gnat who was ruining a perfect summer evening on the Costa del Something. But I guess that all changed the second I jumped onto his back. It was hard to hold onto him as he was saturated in sweat. I felt like a cowboy at a rodeo, trying to ride a demented bull as I clung to his shoulders by the tips of my fingernails. I had to make him stop. I needed to make him stop hurting her. So he turned his frantic fury towards me.

Clutching my bloodied fist, I sat back down and stared at the door, willing it to open. The sounds of breaking glass and muffled screams from within had subsided. I could no longer hear my mother's voice, just my father pacing back and forth on the old floorboards.

I closed my eyes and counted in my head. There was complete silence for fifty-seven seconds. One Mississippi, two Mississippi, three Mississippi. At fifty-eight Mississippi I heard his voice.

"You know you made me do that, right?"

His voice was shaking, his breathing heavy, audible even through the door. I had yet to hear my mother's voice. I scrambled to my feet. I didn't know what to do with the smudges of crimson across my clenched fist, so I added it to my T-shirt.

"I know. I'm sorry," my mother said.

I sighed so hard I could feel my heart folding in on itself like a crumpled origami flower. Just once. Just once, I wanted her to be a little braver and tell him no. Today wasn't the day.

Neither was the following week, or the next month or that August bank holiday when she wore her fuchsia dress and I tried to help her style her hair to cover up the bruise over her eye.

I loved my father despite his insidious erosion of my mother's self-worth. I couldn't help it. I loved him even if I hated him so much I wished he was like an orange. I found that if I said the word "orange" over and over again it lost all meaning and became a strange and foreign sound. I hoped that if I did the same with my father's name he would cease to matter, maybe even stop existing. It never worked.

He always smelt of car oil and Brut aftershave. It was this scent that first defined masculinity for me. When I was younger, he was different from the man he later mutated into. For many years, he was just a gentle giant

3

who laughed all the time; everything was funny and light to him. When he spoke to you, you felt like you were the most precious person in the world, his thick West Indian accent adding an intriguing dimension. He replaced the *th* in words like "think" and "three" with just a *t* so they became "tink" and "tree". The licks and dips added to his charm. His vocabulary was vast despite his lack of education, and he often sounded sophisticated, nothing like a man who worked mundane jobs in warehouses and factories for most of his life. I always thought he had the potential to be somebody extraordinary.

He often lulled me to sleep with West Indian folk stories and tales of his own tomfoolery back home on the tiny Island of St Vincent, in the Caribbean. He loved to talk about the mischief and merriment of a simpler life before he moved to England at the age of ten. Talking about home was when he was most relaxed. At bedtime he would kiss me on my forehead and say, "Night, night, sleep tight, and don't let dem blasted bed bugs bite!" It always made me giggle. At the weekends he would play his favourite songs on the portable Philips stereo and make me dance with him. Each cassette tape was carefully labelled in his swirly, cursive handwriting with 'Soca Hits Vol.1' or 'Reggae Mix 93.' "Come, gyal, whine ya waistline!" His huge calloused hands would clasp mine, and he would swing me around like a human propeller. His soul was at peace when he was submerged in his music and reminiscing about his life on the island, far, far away from our two-bedroom house on a rundown council estate. It wasn't the life he had envisaged for himself, and maybe that's why he erupted and punished us: his wife and child had squandered his hopes for a better life across the Atlantic.

Every time he lashed out at my mother and me, I would swear I'd make him pay. One time when he grabbed the back of my head and held it down on the breakfast table because I had forgotten to wash up, I reached for the bread knife. Now, I was hardly a violent person—I struggled to poke the straw through the hole of a Capri Sun—but at that moment I wanted to push the serrated blade as far into his bulbous gut as it would go. I wanted to watch his insides spill onto the floor. But of course I didn't. I just closed my eyes and counted until it was over.

She was always beautiful, my mum. Tall and slim with wavy auburn hair and freckles that seemed to dance on her pale cheeks. Her father was a labourer and her mother a hairdresser. I never met my grandparents, but from what I've been told they were loud and proud people, well known in their small town. When my mother was angry or excited she would revert to her luscious Glaswegian accent. It was sometimes hard to take her seriously when she tried to discipline me in her native Celtic twang.

My grandfather hated the idea of his daughter marrying a black man. No daughter of his was going to stain the family name with an interracial marriage. Both he and my grandmother boycotted the wedding, and although it must have broken my mother's heart not to have their support, she married my dad all the same and they moved to the south of England.

In the early years, I would sometimes catch a glimpse of my mum and dad being silly in the kitchen, laughing and dancing cheek to cheek by the light of the oven extractor fan. I would peek through the crack of the door and curse my grandparents. How could a love like that ever be wrong? It was only as the years passed that I began to wish my grandparents had tried harder to keep them apart. Even if that meant I wouldn't exist.

Although I silently berated my mother for being weak, I ashamedly didn't try to make things right. He was my dad, my hero and demigod, and I was sure he loved me. If I just made more of an effort to not antagonise him, then I could survive his distorted idea of love. And that's exactly what I did. I survived. Until my father killed my mother two days after my fifteenth birthday.

Chapter Two

The doctor said it was a sudden brain aneurysm. It was nobody's fault, she said, but I didn't believe that. They found a huge bleed on the brain. That word has always stayed with me—*huge*. How did it get so big?

"An unfortunate tragedy. They often go unnoticed," the doctor concluded as I stared at my feet in the hospital waiting room. But I had noticed. She'd had a headache and asked me to fetch some painkillers from the corner shop. I dropped my bottom lip, annoyed that she was making me miss the last twenty minutes of *Home and Away*.

"Do I have to?"

"Yes, Maya, you have to. And I will not ask you again."

She was in pain. I could see it on her face. She asked me what day it was. I narrowed my eyes, unsure why she would ask such an obvious question. "It's Tuesday, Mum."

She appeared to be lost for a moment as she stared into the corner of the ceiling, and then she smiled. "But of course it is." She was dying while I was doing my best impression of a moody teenager.

When I returned from the shop I sprinted to the kitchen, hurriedly filled a glass with tap water and spilled some over the breakfast bar in my haste to get back to the TV. I glanced quickly over my shoulder, looking for a tea towel to mop up the spillage dripping onto the linoleum floor. I decided it was too much of a bother to walk three steps to the oven where the tea towel was hanging. Instead, I reached for a newspaper resting on the side of the table to absorb the excess water. It had that day's date on it. My father was already home.

With tablets in one hand and a glass now half empty, I gingerly edged towards the sitting room. Sand, sea and beach babes still filled the screen but the volume was now muted. As I crossed the threshold into the room I saw my mother sprawled face down across the turquoise carpet. Her dressing gown was hitched up too far on her thigh and I immediately wanted to fix it and save her dignity. I'm not sure how long I stared at her still body, but the smash of the glass of water after it fell from my hand shook me into action.

I had never seen a real dead body before. I had always thought I would fly into hysteria, wailing and keening, but that's not what happened. There was an ominous air of serenity, despite the adrenaline pumping through my body. Seeing my mother immobile in front of me was my ultimate fight or flight moment and my body decided to fight.

I lifted her head onto my lap and then gently patted her face with the palm of my hand.

"Mum! Mum! Wait. Please stop it, Mum!"

I could feel the tears welling but I had to stay focused. As I moved her messy hair away from her face I suddenly gasped and fell backwards, unprepared to see her staring blankly into nothingness. If only her eyes had been closed. I grabbed her rigid shoulders and shook her to revive something within. I could feel her clavicle. I hadn't realised she had become so emaciated and fragile. I shook her less vigorously then. I didn't want to hurt her.

Her body was awkward but reasonably light as I finally rotated her into the recovery position. I touched the side of her sunken cold cheek with a hand that wouldn't stop shaking. My mouth filled with saliva but I swallowed the spit back down. I had to call an ambulance. My knowledge of first aid started with the recovery position and ended with how to place an arm in a sling with a safety pin. I thought I heard breathing and I desperately put my ear closer to her mouth and then her chest. But there was nothing. The breathing was coming from the corner of the room.

I had forgotten he was there. He was rolled up into a small ball like a circus performer contorted into a mason jar. With his knees tucked under his chin, he rocked slowly back and forth with a measured, soothing rhythm. I stood over him, glaring. I wanted to spit the sickening bile in my gut at him. For the first time I felt I had stolen his power of intimidation. She was dead and it was his fault.

"She just drop down. She wouldn't get up," he muttered. He lifted his face to meet mine. Tears streamed down his cheeks and hit the cushion of his moustache. "She just drop down," he said again. "She wouldn't get up."

I sat crossed-legged on the carpet next to her body waiting for the ambulance to arrive. My father continued trembling in the corner, rubbing the side of his head. I couldn't muster any words to say to him. Watching him weep felt like a cruel paradox I would never understand or forgive. I held my mother's hand and tried not to think. There was a game show on the television now. Someone was going to win a speedboat to go with their already perfect life. I felt a burn of revulsion for myself. She had been dying and I was more interested in the ridiculous love triangle in an Australian soap. I could've saved her. I had failed. Now she was gone and I was furious at both of us. I didn't let myself cry until the paramedic asked me to let go of her hand.

*

I opened my eyes and blinked a number of times, bringing myself back into the small white room. It was clearly supposed to look like a living room, but the try-hard décor had a clinical vibe about it. An irritating buzz came from the light fitting. It was the kind of sound that once you heard it, it was all you could hear. I took a deep breath, relaxed my brow and focused on the face of the therapist staring back at me.

"Sorry," I said. "Can you repeat the question?"

She removed her glasses and placed the tip of one of the arms into her mouth. Her mousey brown hair was loosely tied back into a high ponytail, with a few wisps falling around her ears. The brightness of her red lipstick against her fair skin made me stare for far too long at the perfect groove of her philtrum above her lip. I had read all the impressive letters after her name on her website, so I had naively expected a much older lady. Now I couldn't decide if the young fresh face opposite me was a good thing or a bad thing. Perhaps it wasn't a thing at all.

"So, Maya, what brings you here and what would you like to talk about?" Her voice was smooth with just the right amount of sweet. I was unsure if it was all an act to soothe me into a false sense of security. I didn't trust my first impressions, but she seemed harmless enough.

I pulled down at the hem of my white blouse and fiddled with the buttons which usually gaped, but over the last few weeks my boobs had shrunk along with my appetite. I noticed my shoes were scuffed. I took a deep breath, counted to five Mississippi in my head and unclenched my right fist. I was squeezing so hard that I had left a red imprint on the palm of my hand and tiny half-moon indentations from where my nails had dug into my skin.

"Well, it all kind of started with this . . ."

Chapter Three

As I left the artificial light of the Tube station my senses were hijacked by a clash of noise and smells. Since moving here a year ago, my nostrils had acclimatised to the aroma of fresh popcorn coming from the kiosk run by a small Romanian man. He was always smiling, which I initially admired and then became cynically suspicious of. What was he high on? Yet despite my suspicion, seeing him smile made my cheeks swell on a shitty day. The smell of popcorn muddled with the potent scent of lavender joss sticks burning on another stall further up the street, tasted like home. Usually on a Friday evening there were also mists of marijuana and bleary-eyed Rastafarians with portable stereos blasting reggae. The irony of perpetuating a stereotype was lost on them, as they brazenly approached me, asking if I wanted to buy some weed or if they could have my number. Mostly I would laugh or ignore them, or if I'd had drinks after work I'd engage in a conversation that I instantly regretted. This Friday, though, I just wanted to get back to my flat.

Approaching the traffic lights to cross the road, I was confronted with a wall of traffic. There had been protests all week aimed at saving local businesses. The council had plans to revive and modernise the area by increasing business rates that inevitably would push out small traders in favour of a giant shopping centre nobody wanted. This evening it was the turn of the patrons from my local bar to scream and shout and make their voices heard. They were dressed in bright colours and had on fluorescent face paint. They waved placards, banners and percussion instruments, and chanted, "Don't be a mug. Save our pub!" It was impressive to see such a vivid group effectively shut down the main road.

The flashing green man nudged me out of my musings and I hurried across the road. I was trying my best to weave in and out of the crowd when I felt my arm being tugged. Instinctively I began thrashing, assuming I was being attacked, until I heard my name filtering through the din. "Maya, Maya! It's me!"

It was Noah, my flatmate, who like his biblical namesake, had recently taken to allowing his facial hair spiral wildly out of control. He was forever denying the fact he was ginger, but there was clear evidence now.

"Bloody hell, Noah, you scared the crap out of me!"

"Sorry, babe." He smirked, not sorry at all.

Noah grew up in Surrey. His is the type of family who owns horses, wears tweed and will start a sentence with "I'm not a racist but . . ." before telling you a hideously racist anecdote. He was head boy at his boarding school, captain of the water polo team and actually understood the rules to backgammon. But by the time he'd graduated from Cambridge with a degree in theology, Noah had tired of comfortable conformity. He left the manor house bequeathed to him by his grandmother to live in a less than adequate two-bedroom flat above a fried chicken shop. He took a job as a barista at our local coffee shop, which required no knowledge of theology whatsoever. And he was happy. Sometimes annoyingly so.

When utility bills emblazoned with "Final Demand" landed on our doormat, I often thought that enough would be enough and Noah would finally admit defeat. Yet each time he would simply make a cup of herbal tea and say, "So, babe, we're financially fubar again!" We'd both laugh, knowing that our bank accounts were indeed fucked up beyond all recognition, but also hopeful we would claw our way out of it, much like every month.

"Maya, you have to join us!" Noah shouted through the commotion of the protest.

"I'm really tired. Just wanna get home." I exhaled loudly to exaggerate how exhausted I was.

"Just stay for ten minutes. Please! We need all the voices we can get!"

Noah flashed a smile that was always difficult to say no to. The kind of smile that had turned many a night of "Let's stay for just one drink" into 5 a.m. sessions that left me dragging myself to work after a forty-five-minute power nap. But it was Friday and I didn't have the excuse of work the next day. So, I adjusted my bag on my shoulder and headed into the chanting crowd with Noah.

A lady next to me, dressed in brightly-coloured linen trousers, thrust a tambourine into my hand. With a wide grin, she encouraged me to shake it. Noah stood beside me, banging a bongo drum as if we were on the main stage in Rio carnival. His graceless movements made me giggle but I decided to join him in his experimental dance. It released the bad mojo that had been fizzing up inside me. With every wave of the tambourine, I was feeling more energised, lighter, as if this was an intermission in my own life.

It wasn't long before the police arrived. Cheers rang out, not just from our group but from random passersby who were milling around. Around ten officers in hivis jackets formed a uniformed wall directly in front of us. With clenched jaws, they remained still and staunch. The carnival atmosphere morphed into something more tribal. The drums banged harder and the shouts became louder. Gone were the excited shrieks of gaiety and congratulatory glances. I waited for someone to let out a piercing war cry and send a traffic cone and a set of maracas sailing through the air.

People began pushing from all sides of me, and Noah and his bongo slipped out of sight. I scanned our modest crowd, which had now converged with at least fifty others whose faces were hidden behind scarves. The newcomers were waving their fists in the air towards the officers. My heart kicked out an irregular beat as one Rastafarian shouted to me, "Hey, rude gyal! Babylon is coming for you!" as he gestured towards the police. There was more shoving from behind and I found myself moving towards the wall of police officers, who were now raising their arms and shouting at us all to move back. I couldn't stop, and my tambourine now hung at my side, silenced by my panic. The peaceful demonstration had just upped the ante, and being teargassed on a Friday night wasn't my idea of a good time. I couldn't decide if I wanted to drop the tambourine and run or breathe in the bubbling hysteria and embrace the mob mentality.

Now no more than a few yards from the officers, I raised my tambourine again. I was suddenly angry and I wanted everyone to know. I readied myself to commit a ridiculous act of anarchy just as I felt my arm being tugged again. Noah's face was twisted in horror as he shouted, "Shit's about to get real. Let's go! We can find a new pub to drink in!"

Chapter Four

The last time I ran with any intention was during my 4 x 100 metre relay sprint when I was sixteen. Back then I enjoyed running. It was so natural and invigorating to me, and it helped that I was known for being the fastest girl in my school. Running was simply what my body did. It wasn't difficult and I arrogantly lacked the understanding that it wasn't possible for every able-bodied person to run as fast as me. It was a time of my life when playing high-impact sports and being first to cross the finish line allowed me to escape. Imagine doing something you loved and actually being good at it. How things had changed. Now I refused to even run for a bus. The late evening takeaways and binge drinking with Noah certainly didn't help.

I wasn't wildly overweight, just unhealthy. I mourned my slender, toned teenage body every time I entered the changing room in Topshop on Oxford Street. It was like the mirrors and lighting were in cahoots, mocking me over every outfit I dared to try on. I was an average size-fourteen girl with large breasts, thick thighs and an arse that made a generic average size a complete nightmare for me. I had inherited the colour of my eyes, long camel eyelashes and the odd freckle from my mother, but everything else was distinctively my father. I had learnt to lower my expectations when it came to buying clothes, as nine times out of ten, they needed to be altered. It was either strategically pin together the gaping holes of my shirts, or shave a few inches from my boobs with a meat cleaver. Most days, when I wasn't at work, I wore baggy T-shirts, slouched jeans and one of five pairs of battered Converse trainers I refused to throw out for illogical sentimental reasons. Some of my friends believed that my mismatched style and ill-fitting clothing was an attempt to be ironic and cool. I masqueraded as an intentionally styled reject, rebelling against the mainstream and laughing at the perfectly poised, headless mannequins in shop windows. But the truth of the matter was that I was riddled with insecurities about my weird body shape and I genuinely had no concept of fashion.

I hadn't stretched my legs for a prolonged period of time until that night. My brogues slapped up and down on the pavement like tap shoes. My satchel swung wildly behind me as the leather strap dug deeper into my collarbone. I grimaced at the chaffing and it was then that I turned around and found myself alone. My pace slowed and I felt my heart rattling around under my breastbone for the first time. With each breath, my chest ached. I remember my PE teacher telling me to straighten up and steady my breathing after a race. I always hated my PE teacher. With a wide stance I doubled over with both hands on my knees and spluttered so hard that I was certain I would throw up an internal organ.

I then heard footsteps behind me and spun around to see Noah breathlessly clutching his side. "Who do you think you are?" He wheezed hysterically as if he needed a defibrillator even more than me.

"Oi, Speedy Gonzalez! There's no 'I' in team! You just shot off and left me to the hounds!"

I smirked at the drama. Noah had a tendency to embellish, a comedic device I had grown to love. He threw his arm around my shoulder as we both leant on each other for support. Our flat was just across the road and we hobbled forward like two OAPs who'd had one too many sherries at bingo.

When I moved to London I had no idea what I wanted to do with my life. Everything about the big city both terrified and excited me: the Tube, the aggressive nature of rush hour, the impatient glares I received from the woman at the Polish food store five doors down. Damn her and her delicious bread! All I knew was that I wanted to leave my hometown and start a new bold adventure. London, scary though it was, had won me over ever since my mother took me to see the musical *Fame* in the West End for my fifteenth birthday. I was still undecided as to whether it was the buzz of the fast city or the freedom to be anonymous that made me promise myself that this exotic place would one day be my home.

As my mother and I veered around the corner in the back of a bicycle Tuk Tuk, we were greeted with the giant neon lights of Piccadilly Circus. Looking up in wonderment, I knew I didn't want to leave. As I grew older, London became an obsession I had to feed because it gave me the last fond memory I had of my mother. It was the last time I saw her really laugh. And it was the last time I remember her embarrassingly kissing my cheek in public and telling me how much she loved me. Our one day of independence together had forever clung to my heart. Every detail of the day was imprinted on my mind like a favourite song stamped into the grooves of a vinyl record.

After college I had made up my mind. I was London bound to bask in the glorious unknown. I had a diploma in fine art and one summer of stacking shelves at Tesco under my belt. Not exactly an ideal employee, but what I lacked in experience I made up for with determination, good posture and a firm handshake. After blagging my way into a job as an admin assistant at an architect's firm, nothing was going to stop me.

A few weeks after my mother died I moved in with her best friend Mary. My dad was unable to cope and couldn't even look at me let alone look after me. Mary was a divorced Irish woman with no children who lived in a semi-detached house the other side of town. She was only around five foot tall but she was like a Swiss Army knife—super compact, self-sufficient and lethal when she needed to be. Mary was loud and unapologetically so. She was the type of lady who has no problem telling you exactly how she feels whether you want to hear it or not. When she collected me from my dad's five weeks after the funeral, she launched a tirade of abuse at him.

"Just look at yourself! You've become a pathetic excuse for a man rolling around in self-pity. We're all grieving. It's not all about you! You're allowing a near enough stranger take your own daughter in because you're too pitiful to make things right. Get a grip of yourself, man! She may be dead but Maya is still here. Don't lose her too!"

And with that she swept up my bags and marched me out the front door. I glanced over my shoulder expecting my father to leap up and stop me from leaving, but he just sat on the sofa and stared aimlessly at the ground. My unlikeable hero shattered my heart into a million pieces.

The day I left my parents' home was the first time I saw a woman stand up to my father and it felt so good. Mary made me believe that women can be fierce and independent, two formidable traits my mother lacked and I aspired to.

The six years living with Mary were the happiest I had ever been. She made her chaotic home—decorated in floral wallpaper, gaudy brass ornaments and doily-laden furniture—an oasis of calm. The once foreign objects, like the calendar of the Pope that hung proudly in the kitchen and the rosary beads draped over the Bible on the sideboard in the hall, became part of my life.

Mary told me from day one that she had no interest in replacing my mother. She wasn't into sentiment and was a firm believer of sucking it up and moving on. I enjoyed the fact that she gave me enough freedom to be and do as I pleased, with just the right amount of sway to call me out on being "a cheeky little gobshite!" and rein me in when I acted up. Mary never forced me to stay on at school or pursue any sort of a career, and she never used my mother as an emotional tool to influence my decision-making.

Family life started to resemble what my friends had. A sense of normality descended. I had my first sleepover without fear that my dad would crash into the room at any given moment, and friends could call over for dinner without me having to make excuses for my mother's bruised lip. Every Sunday afternoon Mary and I would sit on her weathered velvet sofa and watch musicals. Anything from classic Doris Day and Fred and Ginger right up to the remake of *Hairspray*. If it told a story through song, no matter how ridiculous the dance routines were, Mary was delighted. Afterwards she would stand by the back door with her salt and pepper hair in rollers, puffing on her menthol cigarettes and singing a tune from the film we had just watched. She would be hugging herself for heat, wrapped up in one of her numerous beige cardigans that all looked the same. All the while she would scold me about the dangers of smoking saying if she ever caught me with a cigarette she would "fuck me out the house" and back to my dad's. I never took so much as a drag on a cigarette.

From what I understood, my father sent Mary money to help with my upkeep, but it was never directly discussed. She would sometimes say, "Well, your good-for-nothing father has kept the bank manager off my back for another month," when she was sorting through the mail, so I assumed he contributed. I never asked.

Mary never told me if she knew exactly what went on between my parents and I was determined to bury the past. But she must have known something wasn't right. I guess there are only so many "I bumped into a door" stories you can tell before your best friend called you out on it. My dad never contacted me and I had no interest in speaking with him. Mary was my family now. Although she wasn't an overly affectionate lady, she would sometimes appear behind me and rest her hand on my shoulder when she caught me gazing at the framed photograph of my mother and me in the hallway.

"I miss her too, sweetie. I bloody miss her too."

Chapter Five

It was 1987, the year Rick Astley was never gonna give you up or let you down, King's Cross station was set ablaze, killing thirty-one people, and golliwogs were banned from Enid Blyton books. This didn't stop the taunts of "Piss off back to your own country, ya bas golliwog!" when Cedric Thomas was jumped by a group of men and beaten to a pulp one night. Although Cedric was left unconscious next to a vandalised bus shelter, no charges were brought against the perpetrators, who included his future father-in-law.

Cedric had moved to a small town near Glasgow off the back of a tip from a relative who said there were plenty of jobs going at a local car engine factory. But Glasgow in the 1980s had one of the highest levels of unemployment ever recorded in the UK. Nobody was hiring, and even if they were, out-of-work Scots were always going to trump Cedric. After a few weeks of job hunting, he somehow managed to secure a trial period with a brickie he met while playing dominoes one night. The pay would barely cover his rent, but still he jumped at the chance.

Hoping to make a great impression on his first day, Cedric visited the nearest barber for a trim of his soft round Afro that he swore was all the rage. When he was unable to afford the prices advertised outside of the barber's, he brazenly opted to take his chances at a women's hair salon, who according to the flyer in the window, were running a special money-off deal.

On entering the hairdressers, Cedric was curtly told by a surly looking woman in her fifties, with angular shoulder pads stacked to the ceiling, that the men's barber was next door. She looked like a giant inflatable weeble, as if you pushed her over she would simply wobble right back up and headbutt you. With her hands resting on her bulging hips and an insincere smile stretched across her thin, glossy lips, she was an intimidating figure. But this didn't frighten Cedric. Since moving to the UK, he had experienced a lot more hostility than this. He simply adjusted the lapels of his favourite (and only) charcoal blazer and returned her smile with his brilliant white teeth. There was an uneasy shuffling of bottoms on squeaky tan-leather chairs, which sounded like a chorus of flatulence, as intrigued middle-aged women in curlers peered over their copies of *Woman* magazine.

The weeble-esque lady advanced towards Cedric like an aggressive rugby prop in a scrum. "We don't do *your* sort of hair here," she said slowly, over-enunciating each syllable as if Cedric was unable to understand English. Her perfume was overpowering, and harsh notes of sandalwood tickled Cedric's nose hair.

Still, with his back straight, Cedric gracefully dipped his head, thanked the woman and turned to leave. Towards the back of the shop stood a skinny young lady in her early twenties wearing high-waisted stonewashed jeans and a tight red polo-neck sweater. It was her mother's salon, so she was guilt-tripped into helping out on her days off from college. She was busy sweeping away the dead hair from Mrs Sinclair's questionable blue rinse, when her ears had tuned in to Cedric's exotic accent. She stopped moving the broom across the floor and flicked her long auburn hair out of her eyes just in time to see Cedric leaving the building.

As Cedric walked away from the salon, his shoulders buckled from his rigid stance and fell with a moan. He was trying so hard to keep his upbeat outlook and kill people with kindness, but he wasn't a robot. Little by little his optimism crumbled further with every suspicious look from the foreign white world around him. He pulled his blazer closer around his chest and gave himself a much-needed hug.

Back at his rented flat, Cedric stood barefoot in his trousers and a white vest and stared into the cracked bathroom mirror. With a look of concentration and a pout of his lips, he slowly dragged the razor blade over the stubble of his chin. As he flicked the shaving foam into the avocado sink, he glanced at the bathtub behind him and felt a strange wave of nausea. His thoughts were briefly interrupted with the theme music to *The A-Team* coming from the sitting room. At least one of his five housemates was home. He looked back into the mirror, sighed and positioned the razor blade against his skin again. There was a knock at the front door.

After the third impatient bang, Cedric realised he would have to answer it himself. He threw a towel over his shoulder and ventured across the hallway with the missing lightbulb and down the stairs to the draughty front door. He was unable to make out the silhouette through the opaque glass of the door. He then removed the chain and carefully pulled the huge door open. It was the skinny girl from the salon standing on the doorstep. She was wrapped up in a grey duffle coat and huge yellow scarf that obscured most of her face.

"Hi, I was in the hairdressers earlier," she mumbled from underneath the scarf.

The left side of Cedric's face was still covered in shaving foam as he blinked at the young lady.

She pulled down the scarf from her mouth. "My mother refused to cut your hair . . ."

Cedric remained expressionless.

"I didn't think it was fair. And I was in the area . . . So if you don't mind, I can do it for you. If you like?"

"How did you find me?"

The girl laughed awkwardly. "This town is tiny so finding a man like urmm yourself—she paused—"was very easy. My name is Aileen."

She extended her hand. Cedric hastily wiped his on the towel and shook it eagerly.

Cedric's face then broke into a wide grin and the pair of them relaxed. "Nice to meet you, Aileen. People call me Cedric coz dats me name!"

Aileen giggled.

"So, when will I come see you for a trim?"

"I can do it right now! I have my scissors." Aileen patted her bag and peered over Cedric's shoulder as if entering a stranger's home unannounced to give them a haircut was a perfectly normal occurrence.

"But . . . but."

"Listen, I'm not a professional like my *delightful* mother," she said, rolling her eyes, "but if you don't mind, neither will I!" She followed with a smile and a wink.

"You realise if folk aroun' 'ere see you with me, tings will get madder than mad? I'm sorry, miss. I don't mean to be rude but I just don't wan' to cause any trouble."

She smiled and whispered, "You're fine. Plus, it'll give those stuck-up OAP's something to gossip about at church on Sunday!"

Cedric knew it was love. He couldn't find a spare chair so opted to perch on the edge of the bath. As Aileen clipped away at his hair he watched her reflection in the mirror and followed each freckle around her cheeks down to the end of her nose and around the contours of her lips. For Aileen it was more titillation than love. She had met her fair share of amiable gentleman and each time grew tired of their company. She was far too level-headed and confined by rules, formulas and facts to believe in the notion of fate. The idea of Cupid sounded as plausible as fairy dust, sprites and Athenian lovers high on love potions.

Aileen was a feminist and had recently signed up to the Anti-Apartheid Movement at college. She believed in equal rights, for women and for everyone.

Cedric certainly interested her, otherwise she wouldn't have spent her afternoon tracking him down, but she was unsure whether it was genuine chemistry, the thrill of rebelling against her close-minded community or simply the idea of pissing off her mother that attracted her to him.

Half an hour later, and following a chat about Cedric's life in the Caribbean and why any sane person would want to leave paradise for cold Scotland, Aileen tapped him on the shoulder and announced, "There you go!"

Cedric rotated his head in the mirror to take in his new shorter hairstyle. "Perfec'! Tank you very much. Oh and sorry 'bout da comb!"

One of Aileen's plastic combs had snapped in Cedric's tight curls, so he offered his own Afro comb to help tackle his dense hair.

Aileen chuckled and brushed off the remaining hair from Cedric's shoulders onto the bathroom floor. She left her hand on the back of Cedric's neck two seconds longer than it needed to be there. There was an awkward silence.

Cedric jumped up and went to grab his last folded five-pound note from the inside of his jacket that was hanging in the hallway. He quickly returned to the bathroom and handed the note over to Aileen. She raised her hands in protestation.

"No, no. There's no need."

"I can pay me own way," Cedric said.

"I wasn't suggesting that. See it as an apology for my mother's behaviour."

Cedric tilted his head, trying to unpick Aileen's true motives. He slowly retracted the five-pound note, thinking there had to be a catch to this stranger's kindness.

"Shit!" Aileen glanced at her wristwatch and gasped. She then hastily packed up her bag and headed for the front door. As she stepped out into the cold evening, she spun around on the doorstep to face Cedric who was still in his vest.

"Hey, I finish work tomorrow at six if you fancy a swally at The Plough?"

The Plough was a pub the other side of town, and although Cedric had no spare cash for socialising, he was not going to pass on the invite.

"Sure ting! I will see you then!"

Aileen smiled and her eyes softly beamed as she jogged off down the road.

Cedric felt his chest leap ever so slightly. He had never been asked out by a lady before. It was also the first act of compassion he'd received since he'd arrived in England.

It took Aileen five dates with Cedric to finally declare to her younger sister that he was the most beautiful man she had ever met. Her sister flipped over in her bed and looked at Aileen sceptically. Aileen was lying upside-down on her bed on the other side of the room, with her feet resting against a poster of Boy George.

"I thought you said you didn't need a man and that more women needed to 'nourish their souls' in this misogynistic, patriarchal world!" Aileen's sister rolled her eyes playfully.

"Well, Cedric understands me and encourages my womanhood!" Aileen beamed with a smug look on her face. The thought of being in a relationship with anyone used to induce an irrational rage within her. She had promised herself that she would never allow someone to silence her or pressure her into a subservient housewife like her mother. Yet, there was something about Cedric that made her want to take a leap of faith. There was something about him that would eventually make her break all of her own promises.

"So how are you going to deal with telling Mammy and Daddy that you're in love with a . . . black man?"

Aileen knew her sister's concerns were justified. So far she had been conducting a surreptitious relationship with Cedric late at night, sneaking around behind her parents' back. Dating a black man would be the cause of a scandal. The town was a bubble of normality. Her idea of multiculturalism would be far too modern and radical for the closed-minded community. They would never understand. But she also knew that if she was serious about pursuing a relationship with her colourful lover, she would have to be honest in the end. But right now all she wanted to do was to bask in the love.

Cedric was heading back to his rented room after another secret rendezvous with Aileen when he was struck from behind with a cricket bat. He instantly fell to the ground and tried to break his fall with his outstretched hands. Before he realised what was happening, a volley of kicks slammed into his ribs. He rolled himself into a ball to protect his body but the attack continued, with slurred racist jeers accompanying the blows. When he thought it had stopped, he rolled onto his back and saw Aileen's father swing the cricket bat towards his head. Cedric passed out. He was found in the early hours of the morning by a jogger, covered in blood, urine and various samples of saliva.

Chapter Six

Living above a fried chicken shop had its benefits. Like there was only one flight of stairs between us and satisfying our gluttony. However, there were downfalls, like having to climb over the shop's delivery boxes that were dumped at the foot of the stairs every Friday night. We had complained to Mo the manager a good number of times, using fruity buzz phrases like "health and safety" and "Environmental Agency" but Mo would always distract us with the offer of a free two-piece chicken meal and a jumbo sausage. Two bites into a greasy sausage later and all thoughts of breaking my neck climbing over cardboard boxes were forgotten.

This Friday night was no different. Noah was still exhaling hard and fast as we opened the front door and were met with a stack of boxes. "Oh for fuuuu—!" Noah spluttered as he stepped over the junk mail sitting on the doormat. I reached over to the small shelf in the hall where our letters were laid, gathered the envelopes and stared at the obstacle as if I could command the boxes to move with my mind. I couldn't.

"Noah, go and knock in to Mo and tell him, will ya?"

"Maya, darling, I totally would if I could feel my legs! The build-up of lactic acid feels like a form of paralysis!"

I rolled my eyes so hard I was sure I sprained my cornea. Both of us were far too lazy to make the delivery boxes an issue that night, so instead I began shifting a few to clear a path to the stairs.

Upon entering our flat my body and mind relaxed. It was a small space decorated with candles, fairy lights and mismatched cushions bought from thrift shops and strewn across a thin carpet, but it was home. Noah threw himself onto the sofa with a satisfying sigh and rested his legs across our makeshift coffee table composed of four breeze blocks and a sheet of metal we found discarded in an alleyway.

I made my way to the kitchen, still clutching the post. Various Polaroid photos of Noah and me on nights out were pinned to the fridge.. I threw the envelopes onto the kitchen table and I grabbed a cold bottle of water from the fridge. Even though I had seen the photos a million times, I still smiled with each trip to the fridge and studied every one as if I had missed something the previous million and one times.

My favourite photo was from the night I first met Noah. It was a house party in Soho hosted by an extravagantly wealthy friend of a friend, whose name I have since forgotten but who reminded me of a James Joyce character.

Noah was clean-shaven back then and he sported a rather fetching bright-pink wig and oversized gold-star-shaped sunglasses that night. I had moved to London just a week before and was staying on the sofa bed of an old college friend, Liz, in her one-bedroom flat, while I found a permanent place. Liz was an actress, which sounded glamorous on paper, until I realised that ninety percent of her life consisted of working as an usher in a West End theatre and the rest was spent auditioning for dire TV jobs like commercials for vaginal creams. I didn't get to see her much because of her crazy hours, which suited me as I was used to my own space.

One Friday lunchtime while refreshing my various social media sites, looking for something interesting or simply to procrastinate the time away, I got a text from Liz: "House party tonight in Soho. Are you game?" I looked to the ceiling, pondering, as if I had something other than a date with a microwaveable meal for one that night. "Sure! When and where?" So we made plans to meet outside the Palace Theatre on Shaftesbury Avenue after Liz's shift and then head straight to the party. I remember thinking it was imperative to meet new people so I wouldn't be clinging to Liz as my only friend. I was also eager to have my first real night out since crashing on Liz's sofa, so I made more of an effort with my appearance. And by more of an effort, I mean scraping semi-dried mascara across my eyelashes and going into battle with my unruly hair armed with a hair straightener. The struggle of having mixed-race hair was very real.

As we arrived at the warehouse apartment where the party was being held, my pupils instantly dilated. The contents of my stomach swam with excited nerves and the hairs on my arms were heightened to a level of arousal I had never experienced before. Sure I had been out drinking with friends at home, but this atmosphere was undeniable electric and very new to me. I feared my inexperience was showing, so I tucked it in by throwing back two shots of Sambuca in rapid succession. I played with my hair, checking that the canister of hairspray I used to tame it was still doing its job. Liz was air-kissing unfamiliar faces while I took in the living room. A purple chandelier was suspended from the ceiling. On one wall hung a fluorescent-yellow moose's head, and on the opposite wall there was a giant ornate, gold mirror. The deliberately mismatched styles and clash of colours were enough to give you a nosebleed. But there was no denying that this room was the epitome of cool. I had indeed fallen down the rabbit hole, but I liked it.

The room was buzzing with all kinds of people like a United Nations meeting on acid. Liz tried her best to introduce me to as many people as she could.

"This is Kaz! She looks after front of the house and occasionally busks in Covent Garden!" . . . "This is Gary! He plays the trumpet in a ska band. We should go to their next gig!" . . . "This is Aido. He's a performance poet!" . . . "This is Amy. She's a stylist!"

And the list went on. I was dreading how Liz would introduce me. *"And this is Maya. She has zero creativity or direction and still doesn't understand the Tube."* But Liz simply said, "Everyone, this is Maya! She's just moved to London so let's not kill her dreams just yet!" Liz's friends laughed and held their plastic red cups in the air.

"To the big smoke of opportunity!" Aido proclaimed, and the group laughed again. I smiled even though I knew the toast was full of sarcasm. Even if London chewed me up and spat me back out, it was finally the adventure I had craved since I was a child.

As the night rolled forward, the party filled up with more flamboyant and intriguing characters. The music pumped from a 1950s-style jukebox in the corner of the room. By now I had discarded most if not all my inhibitions after losing count of the number of elixirs and potions I had been pouring into my cup. I grabbed Liz's arm and swung her onto the dance floor, which for that evening was the terracotta tiles of the kitchen floor. We popped, locked and wobbled our non-classically trained bodies to the type of music I would normally be mortified by. After three consecutive songs and unashamed crotch-to-crotch gyrating with Gary the trumpet player, I stumbled towards the hall in search of the toilets. There were four identical doors, all closed. I remember falling through the closest doorway to me and lurching into a bedroom. That's when I first met Noah.

He was lying across the bed with two girls who were hovering over what appeared to be white powder laid out in lines on the dressing table. I had seen enough gangster movies to know it wasn't sherbet they were using. The room was softly lit with a retro lava lamp throwing odd gloopy shapes onto the wall in the corner. It was as if someone had pressed the mute button and time had slowed. One of the young women looked like she was Brazilian, or perhaps Portuguese, as I watched her snort a line of the white powder with a painful guttural sound and then passionately kiss the other girl. Even in the poor lighting of the room I was convinced my cheeks were showing my flustered naivety and glowing the brightest shade of red.

"I'm so sorry . . . I was just trying to find the toilet," I stuttered, feeling out of my depth and suddenly self-conscious as I began fiddling with my hair again. Noah looked up at me from the bed with a goofy grin, adjusting his pink wig and peering over the ridiculous sunglasses.

"Good luck trying to get into the toilets! I've been waiting for the past hour, so I decided to have a little time out in here," Noah said, flopping back onto the bed again.

I smiled awkwardly. Turning my back on the room, I edged towards the door and replied, "Ah, that's okay. I'll just go back outside." But before I was able to push the door handle, Noah was standing right next to me.

"I think I'll come with you! These two coke heads are boring me now!"

And with that, we stepped back into the light and the thumping bass line of the party.

I arrived back to Liz and her friends, who were now draped over a leopard-skin chaise longue. "I've made a friend!" I screamed excitedly and fully aware I was horribly drunk as I turned to introduce Noah to the group. But at that point I didn't know his name, so I left it up to him to announce himself. After overly friendly hugs and slaps on the back, which are only ever acceptable when everyone is steaming drunk, Noah had successfully integrated himself into our little clique for that night. We danced, we laughed and we set fire to shots of Sambuca. I had no shame in admitting there was something about Noah I found attractive. Mainly his confidence and ability to laugh at himself. However, it took just one reference of his ex-boyfriend to shut down any fanciful thoughts of us running away into the sunset. That all seems so funny now, seeing as Noah's sexual orientation turned out to be of little consequence to me.

That night, Noah mentioned he had a spare room going at his flat south of the river, and our friendship was sealed.

Noah's voice droning on in my ear jolted me out of the daydream. "Earth to Maya!" he said as he waved his hand in front of my face. "This envelope doesn't look like a bill! It's from the States and addressed to you. Can I open it?"

I snatched the letter from his grasp. I was sure I knew nobody in America. It was indeed addressed to me, with a poorly inked New York postmark at the top. There was my name, Maya Cynthia Thomas, written in calligraphy that I hadn't seen for years but instantly recognised. I scraped the kitchen chair across the tiled floor and slowly sat down at the table. Holding my breath, I opened the envelope.

Chapter Seven

The Mary Seacole Hospice
Palliative Care
1775 Upper York Avenue
New York
NY 11024
Tel: 1 (212) 715-2378
6/7/2013

Dear Maya,

I'm not entirely sure where I should start with this letter but I suppose the best place to start anything is at the beginning. I hope you don't mind but I got your address from Mary, who as expected wasn't exactly happy about my decision to contact you, ~~but I felt it was~~ I just had to.

As I write this to you now, I'm sat in the bed at a hospital in New York. Despite the white walls and the tasteless food, it's probably the best accommodation I've had in a long while! The doctors have diagnosed me with an aggressive form of bowel cancer. There is nothing they can do and have given me around eight to ten weeks before it's all over. I have found peace with this news. Karma has finally caught up with me. Maya, I had to write and let you know a few things before it was too late. It's funny how the prospect of death is a fierce catalyst to right the wrongs and, my darling, I know I have committed my fair share of wrongs.

A little time after you moved to Mary's I decided to pick myself back up and move forward. I didn't have the strength to also care for you. This was something your mother was so good at and me so very poor. I thought it would be cruel to involve you in my messed-up life and truthfully thought that living with Mary was the best solution. The day you left, I got in the car with all intentions to bring you home, but I was too full of pain to be a real father. I packed up what was left in the house and headed to America. I have a cousin here, so I stayed with him until I found a job on a construction site. Please believe me when I say that I never meant to abandon you, but I understand if you hate me for it.

My happiest memories are the day I married your mother and the day you were born. Your mother's parents were not my biggest fans. It was a different time back then, Maya. Certain attitudes were the norm, especially in small towns, and my black face didn't fit in. When your mum accepted my proposal I was the happiest man alive, but I also knew this could break up the relationship your mother had with her family. I went to speak to your granddad in the hope we could settle things, but the discussion ended badly and the police were called. It took little to no reason for a policeman to arrest a black man in those days. If someone didn't like the look of you, then that was a crime in itself. If you were wise you knew to keep your head down and agree with whoever was in charge, but if you decided to play 'big man' and stand up for yourself, then you almost deserved the beating you would surely get. And a beating was exactly what I got. Your mother and I had no choice but to move away to a safer place. I often wondered if this was selfish of me. I didn't mean to cause a rift. I just loved her so much that I wasn't able to let her go.

You were born in the early hours on a Friday. I remember this like yesterday! You were overdue by a week and we were worried something was wrong. But of course you just wanted to make us wait! You were so small, and those beautiful green eyes of yours melted my heart. I knew right then I wanted to keep you safe. I wanted to make you better than I ever could. I know I failed you in the first instance but I hope you have grown to be bigger and better person than I ever could be.

I have never remarried or had any other children, so apart from my sister, you are my only real family in this weird little world. I don't have much to offer except an apology that I know will never justify the hurt I caused you. I have few belongings and nothing of monetary value will ever be found in my tiny apartment.

The only thing I've ever loved besides you and your mother was a yellow toy car I received for my seventh birthday back home in St Vincent. It was my pride and joy and went everywhere with me! Your Auntie Lou Lou would try and thief it and hide it from me on furniture that was too high for me to reach, but Mama would always come and rescue it for me . . . and save herself a bit of peace! I ended up scratching my initials into the bottom of it just in case anyone tried to steal it! The day we left the island to head to England, I buried it under the big banana tree in the front garden. I borrowed a small shovel from Mr Benjamin's verandah next door and dug a deep hole at the base of the tree facing the house. I remember having to cover up the dusty soil real quick so Mama wouldn't catch me and cuss me for messing up her garden! You see, I wanted to keep my little car safe as I was always convinced that I would come back and play with it again someday. If I left a piece of me there, then I would always have a home. Of course I never did return, so the memory of my yellow toy car is just between you, me and the banana tree!

Anyways, I'm sure you don't care for my ramblings. Maya, my daughter, I hope you have had a good life up until this point and can one day see it in your heart to forgive this old fool. Your mother died before I could fix us, and I hope that this letter is received in good time so I can try to mend what I have broken.

I see you're in London now! How exciting! Are you happy and enjoying yourself? Please feel no pressure to act upon this letter or reply. If anything I just want you to know how much I ~~love you~~ have <u>always</u> loved you. The doctors have me comfortable and I still feel like myself despite what is coming. I would be over the moon if you contacted me but I will understand if that doesn't happen.

You are the only thing I am proud of in my life.

Loving you always,

Dad x

I read the last line and remained expressionless. Slowly folding the letter back into the envelope, I leant back in the chair and pushed it across the table away from me.

Noah silently looked on, clearly aware it was not a time for jokes. "Are you okay?" he asked.

I raised myself out of the chair and with a forced smile replied, "Yep, I'm fine. I'm just going to grab a shower. I need to get rid of this day."

Chapter Eight

The very first time I saw my father strike my mother I was pouring a glass of orange juice in the kitchen. My father had just returned from work and he was silently seething from his day. He mumbled a "hello" when he saw me and then reverted to sighing in such a dramatic fashion that I initially thought he was joking. His face was taut and his eyebrows dipped sharply as if he was concentrating on something important but infuriating. It was no secret he hated his new job at the factory. He only applied for it because it was closer to home and the shifts were less sporadic, but that day his shoulders were bowed a few inches lower than usual. He placed his rolled-up newspaper on the table and threw his navy-blue corduroy jacket over the back of a chair. He rubbed both sides of his head with his stubby thumb and forefinger that were covered in smudges of dirt from the factory. My mother crept up from behind him for their usual end-of-day hug but he shrugged her off.

"What happened this time?" She asked with a playful tone, the kind of tone that sounded like a nursery school teacher asking a tearful, snotty child what happened to their broken crayon.

My father hesitated for a few seconds, rolled his head up to the ceiling and then cracked his neck from left to right. His left hand slowly flexed into a fist and then relaxed.

"Well?" My mother asked again, moving around to face him this time and with a little more impatience in her voice.

And then it happened. He punched her across the cheek and sent her crashing sideways into the cooker. The speed of the contact from his fist to her face was so fast that I initially didn't trust my eyes. It was the audible crack of her cheekbone that made me jump and spill my orange juice. But I remained glued to the spot, silent and immobile. I watched in horror as my mother moved her hand away from her face and a bead of blood squeezed through the gash caused by his wedding ring and then dripped slowly down onto her blouse. She hurriedly wiped it away as if the sight of her own blood was an embarrassment. There was silence for thirty-three Mississippi counts. My mother was huddled on the linoleum floor, my father was still standing but now glaring at the ground and I was holding a carton of orange juice in one hand and a highball glass in the other. The three of us formed the obtuse triangle of an explosive dysfunctional situation.

I grabbed the tea towel that hung from the oven door and leapt over to my mother. She winced as I helped place the scratchy cloth over her wound, but still I had no words to offer her. She merely smiled at me to let me know she was okay and then pulled herself up.

"Dinner will be ready in twenty minutes," she said.

That was all she said. As if the last few moments were a figment of my imagination.

My father finally rasped, "Sorry," and then left the room. I cautiously walked over to my mother, who was stirring a ceramic dish full of chicken casserole.

"Mum, are you okay?" My voice trembled as I tried to force the tears back.

"I'm fine, Maya. Now get out from under my feet and leave your father alone. You know how irritable he gets when he's hungry."

Irritable she said. Irritable barely began to excuse the fact my dad had hit my mum. Was she so naïve to realise the enormity of it all? Or too consumed with denial that she couldn't bring herself to recognise the danger?

It later transpired that my father had endured a day of being repeatedly mocked by one of his colleagues and bit back when he called him a stupid black bastard. It ended in a scuffle and my father was suspended for a week without pay. The manager wanted to minimise the drama while an investigation was pending and thought that my father's presence would cause too much animosity among the team. The other guy, who instigated the fight, was allowed to stay. My father believed that life was out to destroy him and in turn he set about destroying the one thing that already loved him for everything he was—his family.

Arguments became a more regular occurrence. The noise of raised voices was like a vacuum sucking the last drops of joy from the household. It was as if my father's mask had finally slipped. He became an ill-humoured old man with a peppery temper and was only able to communicate through obscenities and grunts. Every attempt to placate him made things worse.

Along with the sudden upsurge of arguments came the profanities. I had never heard the word "fuck" cross my father's lips, but now he used it like punctuation. The one-sided arguments would begin over the pettiest incidents – "Why did you move my newspaper? I was reading it."—and descend into full-on screaming— "Don't treat me like a child! You knew what you were getting into when you married me!"

I always knew by the change in pitch when the outburst would morph into something more sinister. Then I would go to my safe place on top of my wardrobe. The higher I was from the ground, the further away I was from the battlefield. I would often climb to the top of the wardrobe and camp out for a few hours among the giant stuffed elephant my father won for me at a fair in Great Yarmouth, and lie amid the discarded chocolate-bar wrappers. I'd settle down to read *The Lion, the Witch and the Wardrobe* and immerse myself in the mystical world of Narnia until the house fell completely silent and the pretence of my own happily-ever-after would start all over again.

One Saturday evening after another round of unprovoked verbal abuse, my mother came into my room and sat on the edge of the bed. She had tied her hair up and I could see the yellow and purple bruise from last week around her lily-white neck. Her skin looked sallower, and the freckles that once danced across her cheeks were stretched across bone now. My stomach churned with anxiety as I lowered my head and traced my finger over the paisley pattern of my duvet cover.

"Maya, I'm just going to go away for a few nights." She spoke slowly breathing out each word.

"Going where?" I snapped, surprised at how angry I was at her for even suggesting such a thing. "Take me with you!"

"I'll be back soon. I just need to go out for a bit. Look after your dad."

"FUCK DAD!"

"You watch your mouth, young lady! Don't you start getting brave with me, now!" She stood up to face me but I bowed my head, too annoyed to return her look. Then she gently stroked the side of my face and left.

I stayed on top of my wardrobe the entire night and fell asleep just as the White Witch was trying to deceive Edmund with a bribe of Turkish Delight. I awoke the next morning to the smell of bacon and the whistle of the kettle. I jumped down from the wardrobe and grazed the inside of my thigh during my clumsy dismount. I poked at the smear of blood with my finger and felt an odd sense of solace pinching my thigh and watching the bubbles of red escape from the cut.

There was chatter coming from the kitchen as I edged my way stealthily down the stairs, trying to avoid the second-to-last step that was notorious for creaking the loudest. The kitchen door was ajar and I saw my mother and father talking as normal, as if the past twenty-four hours were a cruel delusion. I wanted to be furious at them for this abomination of a charade, but seeing them together made me feel frothy with joy. My father reached out to grab my mother and twirl her around in a light-hearted dance routine he often did when he was in a good mood. But this time she flinched and my stomach flipped with unease.

Chapter Nine

Mary always told me the best way to clear the cobwebs after a day of feeling like potent excrement was to have a bath. But Noah and I didn't have a bath. Whoever designed the bathroom had obvious intentions to include a tub, but must've realised halfway through that this was impossible, seeing as the bathroom was so small you could sit on the toilet and brush your teeth in the sink at the same time. So instead they installed a tiny comedy bath for dwarves.

I shed my clothes, cranked my phone up to play the entire soundtrack of the musical *Rent* and stepped under the shower. If anything was going to take my mind off of my father's letter, songs about a bohemian life sung by a group of young people dying of AIDS in the early nineties was possibly the worst choice. Still, I had a habit of encouraging my own melancholy. If I was going to feel like utter shite, I was taking Act 2's "Seasons of Love" down with me.

To the high-pitched whistle of the old hot-water pipes and the chorus of "five hundred twenty-five thousand six hundred minutes", I began to sob. I hadn't heard from my dad in eight years and not only did he want to connect with me again, but the bastard was dying. Typical. What was I supposed to do with that information? If he expected a tearful reunion reminiscent of a Cilla Black *Surprise Surprise* Christmas special, he would be disappointed. I had built my life around the opinion that the only person you could really rely on in life was yourself, because in the end everyone will leave you or screw it up in a spectacular fashion. It wasn't the healthiest of mindsets, I must admit, but I didn't need him then, so why would I need him now?

Wrapping myself up in a towel, I stared into the mirror hanging over the hand basin. I looked pale, and my eyebrows seriously needed some attention. My mind mulled over the facts in the letter.

My dad would be dead in a month and a half, but what did it matter? He had been dead to me for years already. Still, knowing the precise date was weird. My head felt light. I turned to the toilet and threw up what was left of my salmon sushi rolls from lunchtime. As I gagged my eyes bulged and shed more tears. The heaving subsided and I splashed some cold water on my face. "Pull yourself together, girl!" I told myself.

There was a cautious knock at the bathroom door followed by Noah's worried voice: "Are you all right in there?"

"Yes, I'm fine." I replied, sounding like a choirboy whose falsetto had just buckled due to the onset of puberty. I was failing miserably at concealing my distress. "I'll be out in a minute!"

My bedroom was just a few steps across from the bathroom. The floorboards in the hallway were still covered with specks of purple paint from a weekend when Noah and I decided we were interior designers. It dawned on us only after the effects of a bottle of Pinot Grigio had worn off that painting the hallway purple was a truly shit idea.

I collapsed onto my bed as if I had walked the length of the Amazon rainforest. I was emotionally exhausted. I hadn't felt this way since my mother's death and I promised myself I would never let those kinds of emotions take over me again. I was furious.

Looking down at my bedroom floor and the piles of organised mess, I saw the floorboards I had revealed a few weeks ago. I had decided that I hated my brown carpet, so up it came. It was another DIY job I started and quickly became bored of. The old hardwood floor was now hidden under laundry, a damp towel, books and odd shoes. I propped myself up against my headboard and averted my eyes to the equally chaotic wall opposite me. It was like an avant-garde display of the movie posters I amassed from Camden market over the last year. I had initially used a Jimmy Cliff *The Harder They Come* poster to hide a hideous crack in the wall that the landlord had no intention of fixing, and then my obsession with covering every inch of my depressing magnolia walls with retro film posters took over. *Back to the Future*, *The Goonies* and, controversially, *Grease 2* were Blu-tacked to death. I longed to dive into the world of make-believe for just a moment, perhaps take part in a high-speed car chase, or hunt for pirate treasure, or burst into a terrible song with equally bad choreography. Anything but this.

I opened the drawer of my bedside table, and there she was smiling back up at me, cuddling a young girl with frizzy hair, whose green eyes and wide grin I barely recognised. Before I left for London, Mary gave me the picture of my mother and me that had been sat in her hallway all those years. When I finally settled into the flat with Noah, I decided that I couldn't see her face every day. The sadness still lingered and choked me upon every sideways glance at the photograph. I loved her but I still resented her for leaving me. If I was to make a new life for myself in this fresh and somewhat terrifying city, then I didn't need a daily reminder of what I had lost. So, in the chest of drawers she went. I reached in to take the photograph out but hesitated and then abruptly shut the drawer back again.

Pulling on my oversized hoody, complete with Wednesday night's curry stain, I heard a rap at the door. I couldn't ignore Noah any longer. "Just come in, you big idiot!"

Noah came in and took a seat next to me on the bed. In his hand was the letter from my father. "So, you worried me . . . so I read it," he said.

"Okay, fine," I said, shifting uncomfortably.

"Babe, tell me to mind my own business if you like, but this is pretty serious. And what the hell is the yellow toy car all about?"

"Yeah, you're right. It's none of your business." I grabbed the letter and tossed it behind me. "And who knows why he was waffling about that car?"

"I think you should go and see him, have it out once and for all. Like, he's dying, Maya!"

"You have no idea who or what my father is. That man single-handedly ruined my childhood and killed my mother. Just because he's dying does not mean I have to forgive and forget. He made his choices and I was never a part of that. How dare he contact me now! And how dare you presume to know what's best for me when your family is just as bizarre! You live above a dirty chicken shop in a poky flat, selling coffee for a living when your family are best mates with the fucking royals! You don't ever talk about your family and I don't ever ask because it has nothing to do with me. So yeah, it works both ways!"

I fished around under the scattered clothes on the floor, searching for my trainers. I had to do something to break the tension I had just created. But as soon as I got up to retrieve a shoe from under my bed, I instantly felt like the queen of all bitches. I assumed the lotus pose and tilted my scrunched up embarrassed face towards Noah.

"I'm sorry. That was completely uncalled for. I really didn't mean to take that out on you." I stopped myself from explaining why or throwing a "but" on the end of the sentence, because there was no justification for acting like a bold child. I knew I had "acted the maggot" as Mary would say. She was the one who introduced me to *Rent*, which only intensified my love for capricious dreams in a big city. Despite Mary describing the show as "a bunch of loveable queers dancing and singing about AIDS", we had both become obsessed with the movie and I longed to see it on stage one day. I could picture Mary clearly now, giving one of her mini-monologues on life, screaming at me from the kitchen back door, cigarette in hand while telling the neighbour's cat to feck off out of her petunias.

"Listen, like yer man would sing, 'I don't own emotion. I rent.' It's easier that way. Just like you don't *own* the sadness, young lady. You may feel like shit for now, but don't take out a thirty-year mortgage and live there. Rent it, and when your contract is up, move on. There's enough sadness that goes around, and some people just hide it better than others. So you and that fiery little attitude of yours best be mindful now."

I'm pretty sure Mary took song lyrics completely out of context just so she could shoehorn them into her rant of the moment, but I loved it all the same. Feeling sorry for myself and lashing out were useless. An honest apology to Noah was all that was needed.

Noah lifted his head and gave me a wink. "It's okay, my love. What do you need me to do to make you feel better?"

I adored Noah.

The only thing I could think of that would chill me out was fresh air and a large glass of something with a high alcohol content. I squeezed my feet into my trainers, too tired to undo the laces, and stood up. Pulling Noah up to his feet, I said, "I'm gonna head to the offy and when I'm back, we're gonna pretend that life is good."

Noah gave me a little hug and I glared over his shoulder at the letter lying on the bed.

Chapter Ten

The day after my mother's funeral I woke up with a searing headache. It was the type where even blinking was painful. I didn't know if this was a punishment for showing zero emotion or just because I was hungry. I hadn't eaten all day despite Mary's stern encouragement to have a bite before I wasted away. The service was fairly small, with a few of Mum's work colleagues from the post office. There was Mary, Annie, who would always knock on the door attempting to sell Avon beauty products but instead gossiped with Mum for hours, Auntie Lou Lou, my dad's sister, who I hadn't seen in years, Dad and me. Not one of Mum's family was there. I'm sure if my dad tried hard enough he could have tracked down my mother's younger sister who I knew still existed, thanks to hushed phone conversations I had overheard. My mother's accent would become far more Glaswegian than usual. I enjoyed this. She would then always end the conversation with "I love you too."

I hated the service at the church. It was freezing and hummed of damp. A no-name reverend who rushed through the formalities as if the funeral was an inconvenience, read my mother's eulogy. The thirty-minute service was spoken with a sense of impatience, as if we were keeping him from his tea and biscuits at the village hall. Unflinching and brooding, I stared at the coffin near the altar. Next to me my father sniffed, trying his best to disguise the escaped tear making a track down his unshaven, ashen face. I reached over to hold his hand, not sure whose benefit it was for—comfort for my dad, comfort for myself or just to continue the charade that father and daughter were a united front. Either way, he abruptly removed my hand from his and replaced it with a hanky fished out from his suit jacket.

I remembered my father telling me a story of how one of his elderly aunts at his mother's funeral was so overcome with sadness that she threw herself on top of the coffin as it was being lowered into the ground. The image of a crazed lady wailing and clinging to a casket as the undertakers tried to steady themselves under the extra weight of a lunatic always made me laugh. It made my father laugh too. He said that even though he was grief-stricken, watching the drama of his cousins and uncles peel his hysterical aunt away from the coffin was like a comedy skit. "Typical black people!" he would always say and chuckle. "We always 'ave to make a song and dance about every blasted ting!" As I stood on the grass watching my own mother being lowered into the earth I had no intention of causing a scene. I remained composed right from the first clatter of soil hitting the roof of the wooden box to the last mound of shovelled dirt that covered the mouth of her grave.

Sitting upright, recalling the events of yesterday, I rubbed carefully at the creases of my forehead in a slow circular motion. I was trying to soothe the aching pain like a shaman bestowed with the mystical power of healing. It wasn't working. Streaks of daylight escaped through the curtains and I groaned at the impudence of the sun for shining so brightly. I needed painkillers. I heard the whistle of the kettle downstairs. I hadn't spoken to my father since the funeral yesterday, and the prospect weighed heavily.

Wrapped up in my mother's dressing gown, I walked into the kitchen. It was a Thursday and I remembered thinking I would be missing double PE, which irked me. The school said I could have time off for bereavement. How much time exactly I had no idea, and each day since my mother passed had bled into the next.

My dad stood near the toaster staring at his reflection in the windowpane of the kitchen cupboard. Without breaking his gaze, he asked, "Do you want a coffee?" I didn't drink coffee back then. I never had; that was something Mum would have known.

"No, thanks. I've got a headache so I'm just going to grab a glass of water."

I shuffled over to the adjacent cupboard trying not to aggravate my dad or my headache any further with my movements. The shelves were bare except for a plastic souvenir cup Mary had brought back from her trip to Scotland last year. Her intentions were kind, but a reminder of my mother's homeland probably wasn't the best idea. Even though she loved the cup and burst into a humongous smile when she received it, it made her sad. That's why it mostly stayed hidden at the back of the cupboard. Out of sight, out of mind. Yet, the plastic beaker was now front and centre showing off the blue and white flag on the front with the words "I Love Scotland". The glasses that usually surrounded it were in the sink, which was overflowing with dirty cups and dishes.

The house had quickly descended into unsanitary conditions. Mum would be horrified if she saw four-day-old takeaway boxes spilling out of the bin, the odour of stale prawn crackers and curry sauce filling the room. I made a mental note to tidy up once I had necked some tablets and dressed myself, a feat my dad hadn't been able to do without constant reminders from me. I filled up the plastic "I Love Scotland" cup with tap water and cracked open the foil blister pack of two paracetamol tablets. Throwing down the water and the pills together, I could feel my dry throat twisting to accommodate the concoction. I hated taking medicine of any kind. The haste at which I swallowed made my stomach curdle. I squirmed and positioned myself over the brown-paper bag on the counter, with leftover fried rice. I was sure I would immediately throw up, but after some unsightly gagging and spluttering, everything settled down. I breathed heavily to help compose myself and then turned to my father for some sympathy. He said nothing because he hadn't noticed me at all. He was still staring eerily into the windowpane.

The days after the funeral were very much the same. My dad gawping for hours on end into nothing, oblivious, and me tiptoeing around the house that now felt cold and empty. Dad's usually well-groomed moustache had now spread wildly into an unkempt beard. I did my best to clean and cook basic meals like pasta, and beans on toast. I guess it was a blessing in disguise, because every load of washing up I packed away and every run of the vacuum cleaner across the carpet steered me away from wretchedness. Some days I would yearn for my mother's voice to chastise me for putting an empty milk carton back in the fridge or for ruining her floors with muddy shoes.

On other days, when the sound of an empty home was deafening, I would even miss the raised voices and the crash of objects thrown across a room in anger. As terrifying as those moments were, at least then I knew there was life within the four walls of my home.

The jingle of the wind chime as I pushed the door to the off-licence jarred me back from my reflections. I stood scanning the cluttered shelves of tall bottles for a familiar face. Usually, he greeted me with his wrinkled disapproving smile and receding hairline, carrying a wicker basket full of grapes. It was Noah's and my favourite white wine. Well, it was our favourite when payday was still so far away. We liked to call it being decadent with a poverty edge. The green bottle with the judgemental-looking monk on the label was one step up from drinking vinegar. However, at £4.49 it did the job of getting us merrily drunk as long as we were willing to gamble on the possibility of a urinary tract infection the next day.

Approaching the counter and paying for two identical bottles of wine always carried a sense of mortification with it. Instead of just presenting the bottles to be scanned and bagged, I would feel the need to almost apologise for my poor selection and obvious disregard for my liver.

"It's been one of those days again!" I remarked far too loudly with a forced smile and equally fake giggle.

The girl behind the till ignored me and continued chewing on her gum. I left the shop clumsily, carrying the bottles of wine like a newborn baby swaddled in a brown-paper bag. The evening air was warm, misleading Londoners with the false promise of a summer. I passed two lads boldly wearing shorts. I shook my head in disbelief and followed the orange streetlights down the road. I could see it was getting busy at the chicken shop, as it always did on a Friday night. It would get worse when the pubs started kicking people out after midnight. Everyone needed a greasy fix to stave off the inevitable hangover. Mo's chicken shop was always the after party.

As I drew closer to my front door, fumbling for the key, I heard the raised voices of a young man and woman. There was an irritation in his voice that signalled the start of something explosive. It was a tone I had heard my father use many times. I placed the wine bottles carefully on the doorstep and turned around to the sight of a couple who I assumed were lovers, no older than eighteen having a lively dispute. The pit of my stomach churned as the young lad snarled, "You fucking bitch!" and pinned the girl to the wall by the throat.

I didn't know if it was my delusional superhero complex or just straight-up stupidity that landed me in these situations, but with no hesitation or plan, I found myself clawing at the lad in an attempt to get him away from the girl. I managed to frighten him enough to release his grip but I wasn't as strong as I imagined, and he bundled me to the ground.

"What the hell are you doing?" screeched the girl.

The commotion drew a gawking crowd from inside of Mo's. The girl rushed to her boyfriend's side, checking he was okay, and spat a "Stupid cow!" at me, before they wandered off arm in arm down the road. Stunned into silence, I sat on the concrete pavement and winced as I raised one of the legs of my tracksuit bottoms. I gently dabbed at the specks of blood from my grazed knee and scolded myself through a clenched jaw.

A middle-aged man who was clutching a cardboard burger box helped me to my feet. "Damned if you do, and damned if you don't," he said in a casual tone. "Some people invite dickheads into their lives and for that I guess you just have to let them figure it out themselves, sweetheart."

I half-smiled and limped to the door, picking up the bottles of wine.

I never understood the motive behind my mother's tolerance and forgiveness. He continued to abuse her physically and mentally yet she stayed. Perhaps the line between love and fear became blurred. But what was it about him that made my mother stay? What made the young girl protect her violent boyfriend and then reprimand me for attempting to help her? I needed to know. Suddenly I was certain that contacting my father was something I had to do, even if it made me feel sick.

Chapter Eleven

Tackling the stairs with an injured knee and Mo's arsing delivery boxes was not ideal. Everything about that evening was far too challenging. I placed all my hopes in alcohol to regain some kind of Zen. As I pushed open the flat door, wafts of cheese and pepperoni drifted up my nose. I loved Noah's forward thinking. I fell onto the sofa and closed my eyes for a few lingering seconds. My knee throbbed and my head was mangled with information I didn't know how to process. Noah walked into the sitting room holding two wine glasses.

"Pizza will be ready in five minutes. Shall we get our Monk on?" He nodded eagerly towards the bottles.

I decided not to retell my story of becoming a failed domestic-violence mediator and replied, "Abso-fucking-lutely!"

Three slices of pepperoni pizza later and a bottle of Monk necked at lightning speed, it was all "No, I love you more!" and "But you don't understand! You're my bestest fwend in the entire world!" After our egos were massaged to within an inch of their lives, Noah pulled out his phone and insisted on showing me his latest flirty conquest on a new dating app. Noah never had any problems with dating except for the fact he became bored after the thrill of the chase was over, and that was usually directly after the first date.

"So what do you think? His body looks phenomenal but I'm not sure his face complements mine," Noah concluded, scratching his ginger beard.

I grabbed the phone for a better look and, as expected, the guy he was salivating over looked like a Calvin Klein model.

"Are you kidding me?" I shrieked. "He's gorgeous and you're still judging him! Jesus! Have you ever just liked a guy and fallen for him without sabotaging it first?"

Noah got up to fetch the other bottle of wine from the fridge, and after closing it again he replied, "Yes. Yes, I have. And it was bloody awful."

I waited until he had poured us both a glass and then asked, "So are you going to elaborate on this bloody awful thing, or are we just being overly dramatic just because we can?"

He smiled, lowered the glass from his lips, hugged a cushion with his spare hand and sighed deeply. "I fell head over arse for a guy once. It was my second year of university and my sexuality was the biggest open secret on campus. As long as my family never asked, I didn't tell. But it was becoming increasingly difficult to be a discreet gay, especially when I started dating Aaron." Noah grimaced as soon as the name left his lips, like he'd been punched in the gut.

"We hadn't been dating long, maybe a couple of months, but it was more than enough time for my father to find out and demand I stop making a fool out of everyone. I had become clumsy with my whereabouts when I was with Aaron. I guess love makes you feel invincible. There were only so many dinner party conversations I could stomach pretending I was far too busy with my studies for girlfriends. I wanted to scream and tell all those jumped-up aristocratic arseholes that it was nothing to do with my studies but how busy I was getting hand jobs from various members of the rowing team. But of course I stayed silent out of a twisted obligation to the great FitzClarence name." Noah washed down the bitter taste of his surname with the sub-standard wine. He closed his eyes as he chugged and only opened them again when the glass was empty. He then reached for the bottle from the coffee table for a refill.

"Apparently whom I dated had a direct effect on the entire household. How my blasphemous love life affected our butler James or our gardener Annie I had no idea, but I would've been a brave fool to ever interrupt my father when he was talking, even if what he was saying was pure poison. He screamed at me for hours about reputation, honour and I'm quite sure the words 'Sodom and Gomorrah' were squeezed into his speech. He called me a disgusting fag who needed my head fixed." Noah laughed awkwardly.

"Of course I continued to date Aaron. I, naively, wasn't prepared to give up on love. But my father always had to win. Everything was a game to him and he would bully me into submission. So, to teach me a lesson for embarrassing him and to prove I had fallen for the wrong person, he seduced Aaron. I walked in on them both in the library one Tuesday afternoon, just as the love of my life was performing fellatio on the old man.

Here's to the honourable 8th Earl of Munster." Noah raised his glass in the air as if he was making a toast.

The last few sentences fell out of Noah's mouth as if he was summarising an X-rated game of Cluedo. "The deed was done in the library, by my father . . . with his penis in my boyfriend's mouth!" I didn't know if I wanted to laugh inappropriately, or cry. I placed my head in my hands. Noah leaned further back into the sofa as if he wanted the cushions to completely envelope him.

"So this is why I don't have the best relationship with my father anymore. And because he controls the family, including my mother and younger sister, I only hear from them on my birthday. The last communication I had was an email from my mother telling me my gran had passed away earlier this year and in her will she left me some money and a property. But apart from that, nothing."

My heart ached for Noah, and for the first time that evening, I forgot about my own heartache with my father. I placed my hand on his leg.

"Does your mother know about this?" I asked.

"My mother likes to play dumb and pretend to not see what goes on around her. But behind the bottles of gin and pills for her angina, she sees everything. She knows exactly the kind of man my father is, but she chooses to hide behind WI meetings and organising shitty baking competitions for the village fete."

We both stared into nothingness, just sipping our drinks in the darkness of the sitting room lit only by the cheap fairy lights we kept from last Christmas. The silence was broken with the loud vibration of Noah's phone on the metallic surface of the coffee table.

"So that guy has just asked me out for a drink tonight. Good job I've got a legit excuse to say no this time!" Noah smiled and tapped away at his phone.

"Don't use me as an excuse, my love. If you want to go out and play, do it." I looked at Noah, almost pleading with him to remove himself from the gloom we both were feeding.

"I want to stay here with you tonight. That's what pals do!"

"Well, in that case we're not going to be two sad sacks!" I rose up from the sofa and instantly stumbled, suddenly aware of how drunk I was. My knee still throbbed. I refocused my eyes and toddled towards the stereo across the room. The shabby-looking speakers had been broken and repaired several times after our impromptu house parties. They had a tendency of falling over every time we pushed the volume and bass a little too hard and fast, so were now perilously supported by a few stacked DVDs from Noah's gay cinema collection and a limited edition of *The Lion King*. I searched among the CDs for the perfect soundtrack to the evening. If anything were to shake off bad memories of dysfunctional families, Janet Jackson ought to do it. I put on "Together Again". It was Noah's favourite song.

After two bottles of wine, one pizza and half of a bottle of peach schnapps Noah found at the back of a cupboard and the Jackson family's entire back catalogue, we were both back on the sofa. I swung my legs across Noah's lap and stretched out over a mound of cushions.

This was just what I needed. This was what we both needed—an interlude to the niggling throb of life. Just as I made myself comfortable, Noah interrupted my thoughts.

"I think you should speak to your dad."

With an exasperated throw of my head to the ceiling, I said, "I think so too." Bang went the intermission. "I'll call the hospital tomorrow."

"Or—" Noah paused for a moment, "—you should go and see him!"

"Sure! I'll just go and withdraw a cheeky grand from the bank now! Or perhaps I could fund the trip with diamonds excreted from the arsehole of a unicorn, because both are equally viable options!"

"So, if money wasn't an issue, would you go?"

"Yeah, sure, I'd be flying out on the next flight!"

"Maya, I have money I don't care about or even want to spend from my grandmother's inheritance. You can borrow some and go do something amazing! Don't overthink the situation when you can mend it before it's too late. I don't know what he put you and your mother through and you don't have to tell me, but he's apologised and he's trying. Now meet him halfway . . . halfway around the world!"

I was clearly much more drunk than I had imagined, because I found myself saying, "Okay."

Agreeing to this quest for closure was easier than I thought, and it scared me. But there was no time for backtracking, as Noah had already hauled out his laptop before I had the chance to register the enormity of my "okay". He pulled up a list of flights leaving for New

York that weekend but I reached over and stopped his hand moving across the trackpad.

"Can you see how much flights are from London to St Vincent . . . then on to New York?" I asked, surprised at myself again.

Noah turned to me and grinned.

"Yes I can! Oooh, I love drunk online purchases!"

This was one hell of drunken purchase that made my impulsive buy of a bright-orange space hopper two weeks ago seem almost reasonable.

"Come with me!" I said.

"This trip isn't about me, honey. You're leaving Sunday afternoon at 15.40."

Chapter Twelve

Saturday morning flew by in a haze of planning and haphazard packing. I hated admin, which was ironic seeing as that was my exact role at work. I emailed my boss first thing that morning, shortly after dry heaving through the onset of my hangover. I didn't go into the details, as, quite frankly, I didn't yet know all the details. I simply explained I would be away for ten days to see my sick father in New York and apologised for the short notice. I then hesitated, hovering the cursor over the Send button. It sounded like the worst excuse for a holiday. I didn't want to divulge too much but I needed to make my last-minute-dot-com absence from work seem plausible. I went back into the email and added "my sick father, who has cancer". I didn't want to do it but I did. I dropped the C word. Although my reason for time off was completely legitimate, I detested using cancer as an excuse. Well, it wasn't an excuse exactly, but I felt so detached from it that it felt like a giant lie. It sounded like the classic death in the family, which I had heard Noah use with his employers more than once after a heavy night out. But I was more responsible. And with responsibility comes guilt. In the eighteen months I had been at Rosco and Sullivan, I hadn't missed one day of work. Not even when Noah had coaxed me into drinking on a weeknight and I woke up with glitter and blue face paint spelling "twat" across my forehead.

I hit the Send button and closed the screen. What was I doing? Maybe if I just woke up Noah and explained to him I was too drunk to fully understand the immensity of seeing my father, he might understand. I'm sure there was a reasonably straightforward refund policy on the flights. Maybe if we cited a death in the family as a reason?

I looked over at the letter resting on my bedside table. I read the most puzzling bit of the letter again, the yellow toy car, a totem of my father's childhood that he loved almost as much as he said he loved my mother and me.

I planned to spend five days on the island and then fly to New York for another five. This would give me an additional month at least before I could say goodbye to my father. My stomach lurched again, not just because I was dealing with the acid in my belly from last night's binge, but because I knew I had to deal with another loss all by myself. I gently folded the letter and slid it back into the envelope. I rested it on top of the photograph of my mother and me that I had already packed in my suitcase. Now was as good a time as any to call Mary and have her yell at me for making the biggest mistake of my life.

After six rings Mary's voicemail kicked in, and I was delighted. It offered me the perfect opportunity to explain myself without having Mary interrupting me and telling me I was a "fecking eejit" and how much of a "geebag" my father was. Although I technically didn't owe Mary an explanation, I didn't want to disappoint her. I hurried through my monologue, conscious of being cut off as well as hoping to confuse Mary enough and distract her from the reason for my unplanned holiday. I made sure I ended the rambling message with "I love you!" and "Honestly, I'm okay!"

My passport was lying at the bottom of my underwear drawer. Entwined with odd socks, an array of lace thongs I never wore and granny pants that helped create the illusion of me being three stone lighter in some of my more form-fitting outfits. I definitely needed to pack those. I also decided to take my old bulletproof Nokia phone instead of my oversized and overpriced smartphone. The Nokia was only good for making and receiving calls or text messages, but that was all I needed.

I had never travelled abroad on a plane before. The only reason I had a passport was that most jobs I'd applied for needed some form of ID. I didn't drive, and flashing my NUS student card didn't exactly shout young professional. The passport even smelt new as I fanned the empty pages across my nostrils.

"Why are you sniffing your passport?" Noah asked. He had appeared in the doorway of my room, rubbing the crust of sleep from the corner of his eyes.

"Eh, I wasn't," I replied, hurriedly stuffing the passport into the zip pocket of my backpack.

Noah jumped over the remainder of my wardrobe, which was strewn beneath our feet.

"So are you ready to get your *Eat, Pray, Love* on?"

"Am I doing the right thing? It's not too late to take back your money." I looked hard into Noah's face for reassurance.

"You're doing the right thing, my love. I know you're scared but that feeling will pass. Regrets, however, have an annoying habit of outstaying their welcome. Life is far too short . . . and your father will be the first person to tell you that when you see him."

Saturday evening dragged on in a fog of excitement and trepidation. I finished my packing and finally showered away the remainder of my hangover.

My alarm woke me up promptly on Sunday morning and I felt sick. I instantly wanted to cancel my vagabond adventure, so I ran to Noah's room to rationalise my reasons for staying. But Noah had already left for work. Pinned to his bedroom door was a note:

Sorry! I didn't want to wake you. And stop overthinking. Stop it right now! Go, have fun and keep me updated. Remember – no regrets! xx

I took a deep breath and regained some composure. "Maya, stop being a dickhead," I told myself. I unplugged my phone and began playing a game of Snake as a distraction. Intensely following the monochrome screen with my tongue protruding with concentration, I forgot how addictive it was. The video game inevitably became faster and harder right up until I crashed into myself and died. I tossed the phone onto my bed and sighed with disappointment. Was life as predictable as an old-school arcade game that simply got faster and harder until you ran out of lives? I hoped I could prove my miserable theory wrong.

In my head, taking the Tube to the airport was a fine idea. It was miles cheaper than a taxi, and at 10 a.m. on a Sunday the carriages would be quiet enough to let me collect my thoughts and think of reasons why the holiday had "head-on collision with a faulty airbag" written all over it. However, pulling my suitcase onto the carriage proved problematic. Problematic because it seemed that the entire population of London and Middle Earth had descended on the Victoria line for a Sunday morning jaunt into town. My luggage attracted loud exasperated sighs. The passive-aggressive tuts were deafening. The travelling public hated my suitcase and me and everything we stood for, apparently. Wedged into the corner of a glass partition and with the backpack of an Asian tourist in my face, I cursed the London Underground and everything it stood for.

Finally, after changing onto the Piccadilly line, I had room to breathe. Even if the air was stiff with the recycled stench of a thousand armpits, my carriage was nearly empty, and I had a seat for my suitcase and myself. I opened the side pocket of my backpack to check for the eighth time if my passport was still there. I knew I would be on the line for at least another thirty minutes, so I slipped on my headphones and allowed my guilty-pleasures playlist to distract me until I hit Terminal 5 at Heathrow.

The Tube eventually pushed through the darkness of the tunnels and burst into the sunlight. Chugging along, I found amusement in making up stories for the different passengers on the train.

A middle-aged man in his late fifties sits opposite me. He is called Arthur. He's dressed in a navy pinstripe suit and a white shirt. He has an expensive-looking brown leather briefcase on his lap and he is on his way back home to his wife after spending the night in a hotel with his mistress. He's very handsome for an older guy, so I can see the appeal. In his briefcase are yesterday's Financial Times *and his mistress's crotchless panties, which she planted for his wife to discover. If the mistress can't have his undivided attention, she is willing to break up a twenty-five-year marriage to prove her point.*

Standing to the right of me is yummy mummy Caroline. She's in designer active wear with a rolled-up yoga mat under her arm. Although her outfit and slender frame scream health freak, she drinks far too much wine on weekdays, which only fuels the rumours circulating at work that she's a bit of a lush. She's clutching a coffee cup in one hand and her smartphone in the other as she carefully chooses the correct Instagram filter for another photograph of her baby. Caroline's online profile says she's a happy mother, but the Xanax at the bottom of her bag suggests otherwise. She adjusts her footing and tries to discreetly pull her Lycra leggings away from her prominent camel toe.

And then there's Maya. Sitting completely still except for her right foot, which is tapping gently to the chorus of a power ballad. She's miming the words like a try-hard RnB diva with a hernia. The continual checking of her passport suggests she's a nervous traveller or that she's carrying narcotics.

Just as I began to think up another elaborate detail to my story, the train stopped at Hounslow Central and Caroline moved to get off the train. As she walked towards the door the camel toe in her leggings came directly into my eye line. My mind flashed blank as I heard "Please mind the gap."

Chapter Thirteen

Even though I was 100 per cent sure that I didn't have three kilos of cocaine nestled in my anus, I still managed to act like a dodgy drug mule walking through airport security. I had watched far too many banged-up-abroad shows. My mind was awash with ridiculous what-if scenarios, like what if someone had slipped blood diamonds, sewn into the padding of a sanitary towel, into my hand luggage? Sweating profusely, I was pulled aside, almost certain the metal detector had beeped the word "criminal" at me. I was patted down by a bored forty-something woman who tugged at my bra strap a little harder than I would have liked. She then gestured to my now-immense frizzy hair and asked, "Do you mind if I check your hair?" I simply smiled my consent, seeing as she had already begun. "Okay, you're all good," she grunted, and I was waved on to collect my belongings from the tray on the conveyor belt.

From here on in, negotiating the do's and don'ts of airport etiquette and aggressive families unable to grasp the concept of queuing was fairly straight-forward. Apart from wanting to inflict the pain of a thousand paper cuts on the gentleman in front of me, who was talking loudly on a smartphone the size of a thirty-two-inch television, I was fine. By the time I was ushered to my seat, the nerves I carried from the moment I stepped onto the Tube hours ago were disappearing. Excitement replaced my anxiety. It could have been the vast array of movies I had to get through in nine hours, or simply the thrill of the unknown. Ordering a small bottle of Prosecco felt slightly extravagant, but it was free, and being decadent without having to scrape the pennies from the bottom of my purse felt like canned elation. If only Mary could see me now. She'd tell me to stop having notions about myself and keep a level head, all the while chugging her second bottle of red. I instinctively reached for my phone, forgetting it was turned off. Any texts or calls from Noah or Mary would have to wait until I landed. As I stared out of the window, I felt weightless above the brilliant white of the clouds. It struck me how the further away from land you were, the brighter it became. Everything was so sunny if you got up high enough.

My mother once said she would take me away on holiday to Greece, just her and me. She would excite me with stories of playing on the beaches, sunbathing in the day and eating at fine seafood restaurants in the evening. She spent a summer in Athens when she was a teenager, working at her uncle's tavern. As she retold me stories of her escapades, her smile would light up her entire face. I liked to think this was when she was happiest. Looking out of the aeroplane window was the first time in years that I felt close to my mother. It felt like the closest I would ever get to heaven.

I was on my third attempt of trying to watch the same film when the announcement from the stewardess woke me. We would soon be touching down in Barbados. I wiped away the drool that had leaked from the corner of my mouth onto my inflatable neck cushion. My mouth tasted funky, as the tang of the microwaved tomato-based pasta meal I ate a couple of hours ago still lingered on my tongue. Smacking my lips in disgust, I raised the blind and squinted into the bright sunshine. Initially recoiling like an overly-dramatic vampire, I stared down at the sea and waited for my eyes to adjust. I was so far away from home.

As soon as I got off the plane, the heat clung to every inch of my skin. My hot sticky thighs rubbed angrily together, creating enough friction to possibly set my vagina on fire. As I wiped the beads of sweat from my brow, I prepared to be shaken down by a security officer. But border control was a far more relaxed affair here. I even looked over my shoulder to double-check that a sniffer dog wasn't stalking me, readying itself to excitedly snuffle at my back passage. I had forty minutes before my flight to St Vincent, which was just enough time to pick up a bottle of water from a shop en route to the boarding gate. Walking past the shopfront, I clocked my reflection in the window. The humidity was making a mockery of my hair. I longed for my hair straighteners that were packed away in my suitcase. I poured a little water into my palms and patted my head in a frenzy, trying desperately to control my curls.

Across the concourse, sitting at the gate, I saw a young lady laugh at me over the top of her book. Instantly feeling embarrassed about my vanity, I stopped fussing with my hair. I shuffled towards the gate and sat down in the only available seat, next to the giggling girl. I couldn't decide if she was being rude or friendly.

"Don't fight the frizz! For what it's worth, I think your hair looks beautiful just the way it is!" the girl whispered to me in a posh, boarding-school tone without looking up from her book. I smiled awkwardly and blushed so hard I lost all dexterity and dropped my bottle of water on the ground. She smiled and looked directly at me with striking blue eyes and a delicate nose piercing on her septum. Her appearance was that of a New Age Pilate's enthusiast who enjoyed a vegan diet and wheatgrass juice. I deduced that she probably had a trust fund and lived in a five-bedroom house in Buckinghamshire. The slight sunburn on her freckled shoulders suggested she was not yet accustomed to the Caribbean heat. I scratched uncomfortably at my sweaty top, irritating my chest, as she stretched her hand towards me.

"I'm Olivia." She smiled again.

"I'm Maya," I replied, gently shaking her hand. The title of her dog-eared book was *M for Metanoia*, a word I had never seen before. We were called to board our flight just before I could ask her what it meant.

Despite never having flown before, I wasn't frightened. The journey from London was straightforward and underwhelming without incident. But then I stepped onto the plane from Barbados to St Vincent. The airline was called something so ridiculous that it reminded me of a mango and pineapple fizzy drink you'd find in the "ethnic" aisle of Tesco supermarket. I took my seat, which looked as worn as the armchair in Mary's front room, the one she refused to get rid of because she purchased it for "an absolute steal" circa 1978. There was a torn curtain that was supposed to act as a partition between the cockpit and the passengers, but it was entirely pointless, as it gaped open on its broken rail. The stewardess was upbeat enough as she talked us through the safety procedure, but her impossibly bright delivery didn't assuage my fears or loosen my grip on the side of my seat.

As the plane took off, I could feel every movement as the wind punched the small tin aircraft into the sky. I squeezed my eyes shut, trying to focus on anything but dying, yet all I could think of was the TV show *Lost*, in which pretty much the entire cast died in a plane crash. And those who didn't die had their lives completely ruined in strange circumstances that nobody quite understood past series two.

Just as I envisaged my own horrific demise, the captain bellowed over the static of the loudspeakers: "'Ello, everybody. My name is Captain Reggie. We are experiencing a lickle piece of turbulence right now, but nah worry! We will 'ave you safe and sound in St Vincent in the next hour or so! Please fasten your seatbelt as indicated by the sign above your 'ed. Tank you very much. Have a blessed day!"

My father would always tell me how laid-back West Indian folk were, but I never believed him, after spending so many years around his seriousness. It wasn't until I heard the captain of a real-life aeroplane introduce himself as Reggie and tell his passengers to "nah worry!" that I started to understand the horizontal nature of the Caribbean.

I glanced above my head. My seatbelt sign was flickering on and off, clearly broken. I searched the tops of heads in front of me for Olivia and spotted her at the front. She turned around as if she could feel my panic from behind and mouthed "Holy shit!" at me. I laughed out loud which helped dissipate some of the horror that was causing me stomach cramps. There was only one thing that was going to get me through this—musical theatre. I retrieved my iPod from my bag and began searching for anything with a happy repetitive beat, over-enunciated lyrics and a key change once we hit the chorus. My oversized headphones muffled the sound of the engine, which can only be described as asthmatic. I closed my eyes with my heart thundering in my chest and cursed Noah for making me do this.

Landing on the tarmac of Kingstown St Vincent was like waking from the perfect nightmare. As the plane levelled out on the runway, I realised it was now evening. Neon lights glared from the terminal building, making me blink. I had made it.

Naturally there was no order as we tried to exit the aeroplane. People eagerly snatched their hand luggage and pushed past me, kissing their teeth as they went. It was a sound of disapproval—made by sucking air through your teeth—that I had always heard my dad use when he was annoyed. Apparently it was common practice for West Indians to do this whenever they were pissed off.

Walking into the baggage reclaim hall, my body, for the first time in nearly twenty-four hours, felt exhausted. Staring at the stationary carousel, waiting for my suitcase to creep along, I pulled out my phone and turned it on. The time had automatically updated and showed it was 21.32 and then it beeped several times in quick succession. Five missed calls from Mary, two voice messages and one text message from Noah. I clicked the button below the heavily pixelated screen to open Noah's message: "Hey babe! Hope you made it in one piece without bitching! Let me know when you arrive xx"

The mechanical churn of the carousel distracted me from replying, and I slipped my phone back into my pocket. Twenty minutes passed and the passengers scattered until I was one of only four people still staring at the conveyor belt. Throwing my head to the ceiling, I let out a sigh. Bloody typical! As I readjusted the straps of my bag on my back, I felt a tap on my shoulder. It was Olivia. She was now accompanied by a backpack the size of her entire body and still held her book in her hand.

"No sign of your bag then?"

"Nope! But I'm sure it will turn up," I replied, with little conviction.

"Well, I hope so, because wearing all black in this kind of weather will be a bit of a problem!"

I flashed a weary smile and looked down at my attire, shaking my head. "Yep! Schoolgirl error!"

Olivia winked at me and turned to walk away.

"Your book," I shouted after her. "What does 'met-a-noya' mean?"

She turned around. "It's a Greek word meaning the journey of changing one's mind, self or heart. I'll lend it to you when I'm finished!" And without another word she walked away.

How Olivia was so sure she'd see me again intrigued me. I admired her confidence and relaxed attitude. My face felt warm, and not just because of the close night air but because I felt charmed by a stranger. The carousel finally spat out my life for the next week, and I retrieved the crumpled piece of paper from inside my passport that had the address of my accommodation: Bay View Inn, with its three-star rating, complementary five-star cuisines and views stretching across miles of white sand. It was where the adventure would begin.

Chapter Fourteen

The short taxi journey to my B&B was a blur of broken English and car horns. I was shown to my room by an old, skinny man who seemed offended by my presence. Just before he turned to leave, he stopped to look me up and down as if he was conducting a risk assessment. I felt uneasy, so I panicked and grinned far too enthusiastically, like for an awkward yearbook portrait. He continued to size me up, shrugged and then left without a word.

I had a quick look around my room, peeled off my moist, day-old clothes and collapsed onto the bed in my underwear. The ceiling fan offered a nice breeze but the room was still oppressively warm. Lying on my back, I realised it was very quiet, which seemed odd for a popular beachside location, but I didn't investigate. I had no need to satisfy my curiosity at that time. I remembered to text Noah back to let him know I was safe and sound, but I avoided Mary. I wanted to wait until I was less drained and irritable from travel.

It felt like only seconds elapsed from the moment I placed my head on the pillow to when the sun forced its way through the cracks in the window blinds. I reached for my phone and there was a text message from Noah telling me to update him on EVERYTHING. It was 7.48 a.m. I had slept for a good eight hours but my eyelids were still straining to stay open. I'm sure my body clock would be completely wrecked for a while but I decided, as I was now up, to just stay up and ride out the fatigue.

I looked into the bathroom mirror and found my hair looked like a bird's nest that had just been ravaged by a wild animal. I heard movement outside my window and became suddenly self-conscious of the fact that I only had my bra and pants on. Unzipping my suitcase, I rooted around for a top and tiptoed over to the window like some sneaky but indiscreet villain in a *Scooby Doo* cartoon. I snapped open the blinds hoping to see nothing but sea and sand. Instead, there was nothing but an empty swimming pool and a dirt track leading into a bush. My heart sank. The images online suggested I would be wowed by spectacular three-hundred-and-sixty-degree views.

I fell onto my bed again and rested my head against the headboard. I had less than a week to absorb my father's home country and get to New York. A large part of me resented myself for going to all this trouble for him. But spearheading this expedition was the little girl inside of me who secretly wanted a mini-adventure.

I felt like I was being baptised in the mystical waters of Shangri-La as I scrubbed away the accumulated layers of dirt since leaving London.

The soft spray of the shower slowly but surely reset my mood. After reluctantly pulling myself away from the bathroom, I got dressed in a far more weather-appropriate outfit of a strappy top and accidentally bleached denim shorts from a *Cillit Bang* toilet cleaner mishap. I then hastily rubbed my factor-thirty sun cream into my arms and headed downstairs to the reception. I figured there was no time like the present to go wandering.

The lobby area looked tired and worn, with mahogany furniture and chipped black-and-white floor tiles. Leaning against the wall was an old bicycle and a ladder. A small fan was loudly oscillating but there was no one at the front desk, so I couldn't make a passive-aggressive complaint about the view from my window. I rang the bell twice, but still no answer. My belly rumbled, distracting me from pushing the damn bell for a third time. It was perhaps best to satisfy my hunger before my hangry alter ego got me into trouble. Instead of waiting for breakfast to be served by the elusive staff, I decided to head out into the morning sunshine.

The sun flooded everything in a healthy glow, from the blades of grass to the granules of sand that dusted the paths and tickled the spaces in between my toes. The uneven track from the B&B meandered off in only one direction so I had no choice but to follow it. So far there was nothing but fields stretching out into the distance. I remembered travelling through a town on the taxi ride from the airport, so it couldn't be far. I finally turned off the pathway and came to a junction where I was hit by a clatter of tooting horns and loud music in what appeared to be the centre of Kingstown. I took a deep breath in and, then out, trying to steady my nerves. I wanted to blend into the background but unfortunately this proved difficult. Various gentlemen, young and old, unashamedly catcalled me from the side of the road and from moving open-top jeeps. I was glad I had my sunglasses on so they couldn't see the panic in my eyes.

"Psssst! Hey, sexy gyal! You lookin' sweet today!"

I ignored them and quickened my pace.

My father always said that St Vincent was tiny, so finding a café shouldn't have been too challenging. Nevertheless, in my hurry to hide from the early morning perverts who were acting like they hadn't seen a female before, I ducked off down a small road and got completely lost. On both sides of the laneway were various market traders and their stalls of oddly-shaped food sitting under brightly-coloured umbrellas. I had never experienced such a vibrant clash of food, spices, smells and chatter. I lifted my sunglasses onto my head and strolled slowly between the wooden tables laden with bananas, mangos, sweet potato and funny-looking green things I had never seen before in my life but now craved. I stopped at one stall with a large round lady who had a purple scarf wrapped around her head. As soon as she saw an opportunity for a sale she excitedly invited me to touch the fruit and veg.

"What is this?" I pointed at the green things that looked like a long pepper or giant pea.

"We call dat okra or 'lady's finger'." She replied enthusiastically in an accent that made me feel like I was a child again, listening to my father's stories. "It's a vegetable dat is very nice when ya boil down inna beautiful dumpling stew. Or mash it up with sum dasheen and pumpkin for a wicked callaloo soup!"

Forty minutes later, I had a bag full of fruit now tucked into my backpack and a sticky hand from the sweet mango I had been greedily sucking on. My other hand was holding a sour sop juice which would apparently put hairs on my chest. My plans of finding a quiet café and fading into the background with a fry up had now been replaced by the fresh fruit and buzzing atmosphere of the market. Everywhere I turned, people were shouting for my attention or just shouting because Kingstown market was a theatrical wonderment. I saw traders bartering over a kilo of plantain, sucking their teeth every other second and screaming with laughter over a joke in such a strong patois that there was no way I could decipher it. I loved it.

After I had zigzagged my way through the crowds I found that I had exhausted each stall. Then my eye caught a small bar at the end of the street. It had an "Open" sign hanging at a precarious angle in the glass door, and a neon logo of a palm tree. The sign blinked randomly. I pushed open the front door to the metallic jangle of a wind chime above my head. There were two men sitting at the bar. One was reading a newspaper and the other sipping on a can while watching the news on a small TV behind the bar. I made my way to the corner table, feeling drained but happy I could sit down. As I perused the laminated handwritten menu, a small Indian lady in an apron approached me and asked for my order. It was now 11.30am and all I wanted was a chai latte sprinkled with cinnamon, but I knew better than to be so pretentious when the menu clearly stated tea or coffee were my only hot beverage options. I asked for tea and sat back in my chair. With a sigh, I retrieved my phone from my bag so I could call home. I had no signal, and for the first time since the dawn of mobile technology, I didn't freak out about being cut off from civilisation. It was annoying but I was too tired to care.

As the waitress placed my tea and milk on the table, I asked her if she knew where Georgetown was.

"Wha' ya know 'bout Georgetown?" she replied with a curious smile on her face.

"It's, um, where my father lived," I stuttered, taken aback by just how English I sounded.

"Who's ya daddy?"

"His name is Cedric Thomas."

"Ah, he's a Thomas! Well, me know a Violet Thomas but not Cedric." And with that, the small lady turned to leave the table and headed back to the bar.

I was left confused. She offered me no help or even vague directions. Thinking I would simply ask someone else, my thoughts were interrupted by the gentleman watching TV at the bar.

"Georgetown is 'bout an hour drive away to the north of da island." He said without breaking his concentration from the screen. His accent sounded more American with a hint of the West Indian twang. I thanked him and he raised his hand with slight irritation. I had no idea how I would get to Georgetown but thought there had to be a bus service or a taxi driver who wouldn't notice my fair complexion and British accent and then charge me an extortionate price. I decided I would enquire when I got back to the B&B. Stirring my tea with my little finger, I prayed that the lukewarm beverage would relax my exhausted body and settle my stomach.

I placed my empty cup onto the table and scraped my hair back off my shoulders into a messy bun. The tea was only okay but at least I didn't feel sick any more. Leaving the bar, I felt my phone vibrate in my pocket, telling me it was low on battery. After dismissing the message on the screen, I looked up and saw Olivia on the other side of the street. She wore a loose linen white top with the halter-neck straps of her bikini on show, and some baggy trousers that looked like she stole them from Ali Baba or one of his forty thieves. Before I could tell whether she had seen me or not, she waved from across the road and walked towards me.

"I would say we should stop meeting like this, but this place is so small that it would be weird not to see you again!" She said, smiling. "Drinking this early in the day?" She nodded towards the bar.

"No, no . . . I only had a tea, and it wasn't that great."

"That's blasphemous!" Olivia shrieked. "You only go to Royston's bar for rum or a cocktail full of rum!" She laughed again and I joined in even though I was part of the joke.

"Well, it's only my first day, but I'll know for another time."

She reached into her bag and pulled out her book. "I finished it this morning, so it's all yours!" She handed it to me and, with slight nervousness, I took it from her. It was such a kind gesture from someone I didn't really know, and the suspicious city girl in me wanted to know Olivia's motive. She must have noticed my badly-concealed expression.

"The book's not going to bite you … maybe declutter your mind a little, but it definitely won't bite you!"

I laughed, maybe a little uneasily, but Olivia didn't seem to mind.

"Are you busy tonight?"

"Um, I'm not sure but I don't think so." I attempted to be nonchalant so I didn't come across like a desperate tourist yearning for company, when in fact that was exactly what I was.

"Well if you're free, a couple of us are meeting here at Royston's tonight if you fancy it? Some reggae and rum for your first night in Vincy land!"

I could feel a smile stretch across my face before I even answered.

Olivia mirrored this and began to walk away. "We'll be there from around nine," she shouted over her shoulder and strolled off into the crowd of bright umbrellas and animated market traders.

Chapter Fifteen

I soon realised that the walk back to my B&B was slightly uphill, which pissed me off. A cardio workout had not been factored into my holiday plans. The heavy bag of fruit on my back was seriously testing my stamina, especially in the afternoon sun, as my sunglasses kept sliding down my sweaty nose. Fiddling with my shades and rolling back my shoulders with a crack, I continued to walk with purpose, ignoring the car horns of more men who clearly had nothing better to do. Receiving that amount of attention did not inflate my ego. I was more confused than flattered. It wasn't just me, though. It seemed these men behaved the same with everyone who happened to have breasts. Young and old, fat and skinny, tall and short, the heckling was indiscriminate. I thought it must be a cultural thing as I had never once before been addressed in such a way. Except for maybe the Rastas outside of the Tube station back home. But they were always high on drugs, so they didn't really count.

Finally I arrived back at the Bay View Inn and I felt my body instantly mellow. There was a small gecko guarding the porch that I was convinced would pounce on me, so I screeched and darted across the threshold. Standing at the reception was a rotund woman wearing garish gold-hoop earrings, jeans and a tight T-shirt that accentuated her rolls of fat. She was leaning over the table tapping her pen to the beat of the music on the radio next to her. As soon as she saw me she burst into a giant smile and waved me to come closer.

"My name is Effy! Welcome to Bay View!" Her voice was sweet and more English-sounding than the locals in town. She came out from behind the desk and for a moment I thought she was going to bow or kiss me. That would've been weird. Instead she offered her hand and then vigorously shook mine.

"Yes, Hi. I'm Maya. I arrived late last night. I just wanted to ask about my room—" But before I could explain, Effy jumped in.

"Ah, yes. We have a lickle problem with the plumbing in da room you were originally allocated. But I hope your new room meets all your requirements?"

Well, it didn't, seeing as the Bay View was lacking in actual views. But Effy was still smiling so widely that I didn't know how to explain my disappointment. I would have felt like I just popped a pin in her peppy outlook on life, and I didn't need that kind of responsibility.

"It doesn't matter. And thank you for your hospitality so far."

I lied. Since arriving at the B&B I hadn't seen any other guests and the old man who showed me to my room last night was either mute or just didn't give a shit. But Effy at least was making an effort now and I was far too tired to make a fuss. I turned to walk up to my room when I remembered my trip to Georgetown.

"Effy, do you know how I can get to Georgetown tomorrow?"

"Oooh that's about an hour or so away. You can get the bus from town but I'm not sure of the times. Or if you really want to take in this beautiful island, then get a scooter or motorbike! My cousin Leebut next door has one you can hire for the day."

I laughed out loud and then noticed Effy's expressionless face. Was she serious? Being spontaneous and facing my fears was one thing, but killing myself was quite another. "Thanks, Effy, I'll think about it and get back to you." I forced a smile and continued walking up the wooden steps to my room.

I was greeted with a towel formed in the shape of a swan resting neatly on top of my freshly made bed. There was nothing like fresh sheets to entice me into a slumber. I offloaded the bag of fruit into the mini fridge and began peeling my damp clothes from my skin. I stripped off my top, whacking the fan on full blast and walked into the bathroom, with the leg of my shorts still dragging along the wooden floor by my ankle. Even the act of removing clothing seemed too bothersome. I let out a satisfying sigh, feeling the cool tiles on my bare feet, and then splashed water onto my face. Even though I had only been out in the sun for a few hours, I had noticed one thing: My freckles that laid dormant for years in cold grey England were now jumping and waving enthusiastically from my face.

I attempted to plug my phone in to charge it and realised I would need to perform some sort of engineering experiment so the plug wouldn't fall out of the wonky wall socket. My phone charger and adapter hung at an odd angle from the two holes in the wall, with little support, so I tried to use my sun cream bottle as a counterweight to stabilise it. With just enough science and a wiggle from the lead, my phone burst into action again. I waited for a while for the signal to regulate but still it refused to settle. Waving the handset above my head was also fruitless. My 2004 Nokia may have been the old reliable, but I would've offered a severed limb to the gods for a phone with Wi-Fi right then. Well at least Noah knew I had arrived, and when I ventured out later I would try and find a spot with a signal to listen to Mary's voice messages.

Spread-eagled on top of the new bed sheets, I began flicking through the pages of Olivia's book, *Metanoia*. Words like "spiritual", "mind", "soul" and "healing" jumped out at me. I had never read a self-help book before, mainly because I thought they were one big con. "Bollocks!" I tossed the book aside and breathed out my irritation.

The sound of Aretha Franklin's "Respect" dragged me out of my sleep and I felt around on the bedside table to find my phone. It was my signature alarm that used to help me face college. It was supposed to make me feel empowered, but most days the only liberation I felt was throwing my phone across the room in a sleepy rage. I managed to tap a button to shut off the alarm, and the sun cream bottle fell onto the floor along with the charger. The screen read 5 p.m. and I now had a full battery, but still no signal. I shimmied up the bed and waited for my eyes to adjust. Forcing myself to squint, I realised the sensation of motion sickness had completely vanished. Maybe the three-hour sleep helped acclimatise me to my new surroundings.

Peering out from my window, I could see the sun beginning to set. For a room with no view, it wasn't so bad. The sounds of crickets and slow, passing traffic filled the air as the sun squeezed out the last streak of orange from behind the fields. Granted there was no white sand or waves crashing onto the shore, but it sure beat looking out onto the piss heads congregating around Mo's chicken shop. The rumble in my stomach reminded me I had hardly eaten today and I wanted to grab some food before meeting Olivia later. The drumroll in my stomach also told me I was nervous.

There was a restaurant at the B&B, but by restaurant I mean a patio area with some plastic garden furniture and Effy in a small kitchen. I pulled on some tracksuit bottoms and a baggy T-shirt before dousing myself in mosquito repellent and headed downstairs to the dulcet tones of Effy singing. It was an upbeat rendition of a church hymn, complete with improvised handclaps and an irregular but tuneful mumble to fill the blanks of the words she clearly didn't know. Her carefree attitude made me smile.

I sat on the plastic chair and watched a trail of ants work their way down the steps of the patio towards the derelict swimming pool. Effy bounded over to me with a huge grin and handed me the menu.

"How was your sleep?" she asked.

"It was amazing, thanks! I feel refreshed, ready to hit the town!" I said, trying to match Effy's energy.

"Well, just you be careful on your own tonight. There's some idiot lickle boys out there who like to think they're big man. Just ignore them and stick with people you know."

I appreciated Effy's words of warning but I had spent most of my life battling idiot men who felt that just because I had a vagina I was weaker than them. Also, Noah made me pack a rape alarm, just in case.

"Don't worry, Effy, I'll be sure to be safe and stay with my friends." I talked as if I had a whole gang of mates to meet.

"What brings you to St Vincent?" Effy asked.

I shifted nervously in my seat. "My dad grew up here so I just thought I'd come out and visit the place for a holiday." It wasn't a lie.

I scanned the menu, closing down the conversation, and finally decided on the dish of the day: fried fish and dumpling. Two items of food I had never sampled together but I was interested to taste. Effy skipped off back to the kitchen and quickly returned to the table with a large ceramic plate overflowing with provisions. Each ingredient complemented the other and I was surprised at how such simple ingredients could conjure up such a lip-smacking flavour. It was the day my taste buds fell in love with Effy.

Chapter Sixteen

Pouring myself into the tummy-control granny pants proved trickier than usual, especially after Effy's exquisite dinner. I was stuffed and the food baby I was carrying made even walking up the stairs a challenge. Finally, wearing a blue floral maxi dress, I stepped back from the mirror. I wondered what it was about being abroad that made wearing such ridiculous items of clothing plausible. I rarely wore dresses back home, but Noah made me pack one "just in case". I attempted to spruce up my appearance by trailing my index finger, dabbed in bronze eye-shadow, across my eyelids. I was certain I resembled a pantomime dame, but it was already 8.30, so there was no time to start again.

Twenty-five minutes later I was back in town. I didn't have any small coins on me, so I handed a crisp $20 note to the taxi driver and sat patiently in the back seat awaiting my change. But he took so long trying to find the correct denominations of coins and notes that in the end I croaked, "Keep the change." I was sure it was a ploy to bleed a few dollars out of a tourist, but I was far too concerned with fussing with the way my dress fell around my body to cause drama. Stepping out of the cab, I was faced with the epilepsy-inducing neon light of the palm tree at Royston's bar. It was a lot more uncomfortable on the eyes in the dark. With a deep breath, I opened the door and was instantly enveloped by a warm blanket of reggae music. The bar had filled up considerably since lunchtime and I found myself contorting my body through the crowds just to get to the bar. I glanced at a cocktail menu wedged between two beer bottles and pointed to the first one that had the word rum in its name.

I quickly scanned the room but couldn't see Olivia. This could be awkward. I had no way of reaching her, so I decided if she didn't arrive in the next fifteen minutes, I would down my drink and head back. Having a tea or a spot of lunch on your own was totally acceptable, but drinking alone in a bar just seemed too embarrassing for me. The barman handed me my drink, adorned with fruit and tropical-themed accessories hanging from the side of the glass. I took a sip and immediately felt the rum warm my chest. He gave me a thumbs-up with a gleaming smile. I clenched my jaw through the embers that now seemed to be burning in my ribcage and returned the thumbs-up. I manoeuvred my way from the bar area to a high table and casually rested my arm against it. I took my phone from my bag and attempted to conjure up a signal by hopelessly shaking it, but still my screen had "No service" stamped across it. It was 9.05 p.m.

I wasn't sure if it was the bassline coming from the speakers or the fact that I necked most of my drink at an alarming speed, but I found myself bopping my head to the music. There's something about reggae that sends a rush of blood to the head. It made my body involuntarily twitch in such a way that if I stopped moving it almost felt sacrilegious.

My mind floated back to when I was younger, before life descended into madness. My dad always found delight playing reggae classics from his little stereo, by the likes of Bob Marley to Jimmy Cliff, Toots and the Maytals and Desmond Dekker. I would watch him raise his hands in the air and wiggle his waist, joyful movements that I would mimic. We would twist and turn all through the house like a human train on a track, bouncing to every song, with me trying desperately to keep up. The only respite we had was when we would fall about laughing together.

The tap on my shoulder spun me out of my daydream and I turned to see Olivia. I missed the first few words from her mouth, but that didn't matter as she suddenly gave me hug. She was dressed in a simple white Rolling Stones T-shirt and blue skinny jeans. I felt stupidly overdressed.

"Have you been waiting long?" she shouted over the music.

"No," I lied.

Beside her stood a tall skinny lad with messy blond hair and glasses. Olivia had her arm around his waist.

"This is Tom. We both work on the conservation project down by the port." Tom stretched his long arm towards me and I shook his hand.

"Same again?" Tom asked, pointing to my empty glass.

"Yes, please," I said with a forced smile.

Tom gave Olivia a wink and then cut through the crowd towards the bar.

"I'm so glad you made it!"

"Well, I had to check out the rum and music!" I replied, now feeling slightly more relaxed. "So you work here on the island?"

"Yes! I'm volunteering with a few guys, including Tom."

I nodded but couldn't help thinking why I might be the third wheel on a night out.

"So what brings you here?"

"My father grew up here, so I just fancied a little holiday before I head to New York at the end of the week."

I could see Olivia's eyes spark, as if she was impressed with my travel plans. I was painting myself as an international jetsetter, but I didn't know how else to answer. Tom planted my glass of the fruity rum concoction on the table and handed Olivia a bottle of beer. I felt rather silly with my flamboyant cocktail and floaty dress. All I needed was a set of castanets and I would have looked like a giant dancing flamenco prick. I hastily removed the pineapple chunk and tiny, neon green pirate sword from my drink. Olivia must have caught my embarrassment and gave me a reassuring smile.

The evening escalated rapidly as the rum blew apart my inhibitions. The music pumped harder and faster as reggae flowed into high-octane soca music. I felt as if I was at a Zumba class like the one Noah dragged me to one Wednesday evening, but I was actually enjoying myself this time. Tom very quickly became my new favourite person as he struggled to contain himself after a couple of bottles of beer. He was off on the dance floor dancing by himself and high-fiving everyone who walked past him. Olivia and I giggled as he performed the robot dance for a group of ladies who were howling with laughter at him.

"Are you and Tom together?" I asked Olivia disregarding how forward or personal I might sound.

She laughed out loud, putting her hand over her mouth as not to spit out her drink. "Oh, God no! Tom and I are just mates. He's over here on his own like me, so we kind of clicked from the get-go. Why do you ask?" She smiled at me with one raised eyebrow.

I was unsure if she was teasing me, so I just said, "Oh no reason . . . I just was wondering." I looked down into my drink and sucked hard on my straw, but I could still feel her eyes on me.

Olivia grabbed my hand and pulled me onto the dance floor. I was startled at first, still sucking heavily on the straw in my glass, but before I knew it, I was throwing my arms in the air and executing some imaginative moves among the other sweaty bodies. My feet were being trampled on, mainly by Tom, but like Mr Bob Marley said himself, "One good thing about music, when it hits you, you feel no pain." So, despite Tom's lack of awareness for my open-toe sandals, I danced on.

Each infectious song blended effortlessly into the next. I leaned into Olivia's ear to tell her I needed some air and would be back. Pushing through the door, I felt as if someone had boxed me in the stomach. It still felt balmy outside but the night air licked me sideways, rolling over my rum-soaked belly. I was aware there were people hanging around outside the bar and I didn't want to appear as intoxicated as I felt, so I threw my shoulders back in an attempt to steady myself. The thud of the music from inside was beating in time with my heart. I could hear the blood pumping in my ear. I needed to sit down. I found a broken brick wall on the opposite side of the road and perched there for a moment, trying to stabilise my breathing. I took my phone from my bag and narrowed my eyes to focus on the screen. The numbers seemed fuzzy but I could just make out it was 1.47 a.m.

I wanted to speak to Noah. I needed the familiarity of a friend to anchor me. I waved the phone above my head, but still the signal icon had a red strike through it. "For God's sake!" I exclaimed loudly. A few bystanders chatting with drinks and cigarettes in hand turned around to see what I was shouting about. I passively raised my hand as a way of an apology.

"Sorry, everyone! It's just that my phone is totally shit!"

Nobody cared; I was just another drunken reveller. I decided that maybe if I walked in another direction the signal would improve. I hoisted myself up from the wall and floated away from the bar, towards the harbour. It was quiet and calm with few streetlights. As I neared the water I saw the moonlight ripple across the surface. The sparkling glow reminded me of the Christmas lights on Regent Street. I squinted at my phone again. "Damn it!" I shouted. There was laughter from behind me as two young lads approached.

"Hey, gyal! Whatcha doin' down 'ere so?" a guy wearing a yellow vest and baggy jeans asked, with a smile

I didn't feel comfortable with. His friend was shorter and wearing a T-shirt that was at least three sizes too small. I couldn't decide which was worse, the outline of his man boobs or the hideous gold chain that swung around his tree-trunk neck.

"I'm . . . um . . . just leaving," I replied shakily, not just because I was drunk but mostly because I was scared.

The shorter guy was staring at my cleavage. I instinctively raised the top half of my dress. As I attempted to stride forward, the taller man blocked my path, guiding me backwards out of view of the main road.

"I said, little lady, wha' ya doin' down 'ere . . . all alone? And what have you got down dere for me?" He motioned towards my breasts. His voice sounded more urgent. My mind swirled with panic. How would I retrieve my rape alarm from my bag without them seeing? The closer he got, the clearer his crooked teeth and hideous gold fillings were. His smile twisted. I planted my feet in the ground and made the decision to run if they came any closer. They advanced and I saw the shorter guy lick his fat lips. I held my breath. One Mississippi, two Mississippi, three Mississippi and then suddenly there was another man's voice.

"She's not here on her own . . . so move your rasclart before I thump out your dutty teeth!"

Chapter Seventeen

There was commotion and the sound of feet scuttling away like rodents inside a drainpipe, but I daren't open my eyes. I felt a large hand on my arm and shrieked as I stumbled backwards.

"It's okay! Chill out. I'm not going to hurt you." I opened my eyes and in front of me stood the man from the bar at lunchtime, the one who told me where Georgetown was. My body relaxed.

"You shouldn't be down here on your own. Not at this time of night." His face had flecks of black and grey stubble and wore a stern expression, as if he were reprimanding a child. His breath smelt of stale tobacco but it was a welcome stench after my brush with stupidity.

"Are you all right, gal?" he asked, more softly this time.

"Yes, yes . . . I am so sorry! Thank you so, so much. I don't know what I would've done if you weren't here. I just wanted my phone to work."

"Well there was a storm at the weekend that mashed up some telephone masts, so that's why the mobile signal is a little broken right now. And dem boys wouldn't have been nice . . . your body would probably be floating out to sea come morning."

I laughed nervously, unsure if he was joking. I glanced out onto the water and felt sick.

"Let's get you back to the bar. A shot of rum will sort you out!" He half smiled at me.

"Do you mind if I just sit for a moment? I need to catch my breath a little." My voice was still shaking as I lowered myself onto a bench directly under a lamppost.

"Well, I guess I have to stay now." He cautiously sat down beside me, lit a cigar retrieved from his shirt pocket and looked up to the night sky.

I had encountered many men in London who thought it was their God-given right to either touch me inappropriately or to address me in a derogatory manner, but being so far away from home made me feel vulnerable. I was out of my depth, and being dressed in a more revealing outfit than I was used to didn't help. I felt safer in my armour of baggy T-shirts and ill-fitting jeans.

No. Wait. I tried to stop my septic train of thought by shaking my head. It was a ridiculous notion to think I was blaming the lines, curves and folds of my body for the harassment instead of pointing the finger at the real offenders. My femininity and outfit choice did not indicate consent or to be treated as a sexual object. It made me feel gross. I couldn't decide if I was furious or just wanted to stay still and cry my little heart out. But I had company, so I didn't want to freak him out by blubbing uncontrollably.

The man sitting next to me was still looking up into the inked sky. Under the glow of the streetlight I couldn't help but notice the layer of chest hair, laid like a shredded moleskin rug, poking out of the top of his loose shirt. I pondered whether the lack of buttons and plunging neckline were necessary. It was a weird hybrid of wanting to be topless but being too self-conscious to commit to a full bare chest. He impatiently tapped his toes in his leather-strapped sandals and let out a long exasperated sigh. Still, his company instilled an odd sense of comfort. He had after all just rescued me from some unsavoury animals masquerading as men, so I believed I was in safe hands.

"You can go if you like," I said, but secretly hoped he would stay.

"On a night like tonight with a full moon, you might not only be bothered by lickle fools. I'm pretty sure there's duppy down 'ere just waiting for a nice English girl like you!" He smiled to himself, breathed out a plume of thick cigar smoke and gave me a sly sideways glance.

"Duppy?" I asked, bemused.

"Nobody tell ya 'bout jumbee story . . . and tings that go bump in da night? La Diablesse, the she-devil with her cloven hoof, or Loup Garou who changes into a wild beast . . . or Labelle . . . Ronx?" The man became more animated with every word he spoke. I shook my head, confused. He rolled his eyes.

"Well, a duppy is a ghost. And in da Caribbean, there are many tales of da supernatural world. There's a local legend that La Diablesse walks da harbour at night, enticing young sailors with her captivating beauty. To look at her you would tink that she is a shy, beautiful lady, but her wide-brimmed hat hides her monstrous face, and her long dress conceals her hoof. But when her victim discovers her true nature, it's too late! She done leave dem fi dead! Some people tink it's a joke, but the only joke is on da person who doesn't believe!" He chuckled to himself and I began to question how safe I really was.

"I'm not really a fan of ghost stories," I said, disturbed by the possibility that a she-devil could accost me at any given moment.

"My father used to tell me Anansi stories as a child. I guess I was too young for jumbee stories! He would swap the traditional happily-ever-after fairy tales my mother tried to encourage for funny little stories about the trickster Brer Rabbit and Tar Baby. I even had a pet spider I caught in the garden one summer and named him Anansi. My dad thought it was hilarious but my mum screamed and made me set it free . . ." I trailed off and fiddled with the strap of my dress.

"Ah yes! The great oral tradition is big for Vincy folk. A lot of old men and women sit around, drink plenty rum and talk a whole heap of fart all day long . . . or at least until the food and drink runs out! It was nice that your daddy passed that onto you."

I said nothing. The thought of my father imparting any form of wisdom or culture sounded absurd.

"Do you get to see ya daddy a lot?"

"He doesn't live close anymore." I hoped that would be the end of it.

"Well next time you see him, sit down with him and give him some time. Sometimes us old boys just want time with our children before it's too late. Let him tell you more 'nansi stories. You young people tink you are smart, but you still don't know da first ting about where you come from."

I felt like I was being disciplined by an elder.

"So how long have you been living here?" I asked with a peppy tone, changing the subject. The man's accent wasn't as strong as the other locals and it was muddled with American shades, so I assumed he wasn't a native.

The man looked at his watch in an exaggerated movement, like a mime artist trying to convey exactly how impatient he was.

"About twelve years ago."

I continued to stare at him, awaiting more information.

"You love fi talk, eh?" he said with an air of annoyance now the questions were directed at him, but I didn't care and I wasn't going to let him escape the conversation any time soon. "I'm originally from Philadelphia but after my divorce I decided I wanted more sunshine and less stress. So here I am!"

"And do you miss it?"

"The only ting about da place I miss is my son." He rolled his head back up to the starry sky again and sucked long and hard on the diminishing stub of his cigar. There was obvious pain in his face at the mention of his son. I knew too well how talking about family wasn't easy.

We remained silent for seventeen Mississippi counts as I listened to the puffs of his cigar and the music from the bar in the distance. I tilted my head to the heavens, squinted with one eye and focused on the brightest star. The only thing I missed about my hometown was my mother. I always wanted to escape to London but if I was honest with myself, after she died I just wanted to escape the memories of her. Even if Mary hadn't liberated me from my father, I wouldn't have been able to stay in that house. The scent of her perfume lingered for days after her funeral. It permeated every room in the house. As soon as I felt that the smell was fading, I would spray the perfume onto her bathrobe and wrap myself in it at night. Although my home was a minefield of chaos and pain, it was also full of memories of boundless fun and laughter. I plummeted into adulthood the day after she died like a terrified child on a faulty helter-skelter. I wished I savoured the moments for just one Mississippi longer before they became nothing but fuzzy memories.

The noise of gravel rubbing against itself stirred me away from my star-gazing. The man shuffled his sandals on the shingle underneath the bench and leaned forward, his hands dangling between the wide spread of his legs.

"He would have been eighteen on Monday," he whispered.

Past tense. I said nothing.

"If there's one ting you should promise yourself in life, it should be to appreciate what ya 'ave now before it's too late. Death is the one ting in dis world dat is inevitable, but we will never ever be prepared for it."

I was far too intoxicated for deep-and-meaningfuls with a stranger but I found myself enthralled. The man was uncomfortably on point. It felt as if someone was poking me with a thousand needles. With a deep sigh, I rose from the bench and brushed down the front of my dress.

"Shall we go back now?"

The man stubbed out his cigar on the ground and slowly got up. He then led the way back to the lights of the main road and I closely followed, too frightened to be left alone to be stolen away by the woman with the cloven hoof.

Chapter Eighteen

When we arrived at the bar I saw Olivia standing on her own. A mix of embarrassment and relief made my heart beat faster.

"Maya! There you are!" She waved her hand and ran over to me like an excitable Andrex puppy. "Royston! What are you doing here?" she screeched at my hero.

"You're Royston?" I asked, blinking furiously as it began to dawn on me. I hadn't even asked his name.

He nodded with an air of nonchalance.

"So this must be your bar?"

Again, he dipped his head as if my question was pointless.

Olivia looked on, puzzled but still swigging from a bottle of beer.

Royston turned to Olivia and warmly said, "I was simply saving a damsel in distress. When you're both done out 'ere, come in and get sumting to drink." He gave me a small smile and walked back into the bar.

"What the hell was all that about?" Olivia asked suspiciously.

"Oh, nothing . . . I just met him down at the harbour." I didn't want to retell my mini-drama out of shame for having got myself into such a horrible situation. "He seems nice but odd!"

"That's Royston for you! When it comes to talking about himself, he's a man of few words, but when he does speak, it's worth listening. And sometimes you feel like you need to apologise even though you're not entirely sure why. Some people think he's rude but I think there's something captivating about him." Olivia lowered her voice. "His son was killed in a car accident when he was only six-years-old which may explain why he gives zero fucks about everyone and thing."

I felt a sudden throb of sadness for Royston.

I watched Olivia look affectionately towards the bar. Was it his speckled grey stubble, the layer of fur on his chest, or his blasé attitude that did it for her? Whatever it was, I found myself feeling ripples of jealousy I was not prepared for, and seeing Olivia swoon over my champion for the evening was pissing me off.

"So riddle me this, do you have a thing for Royston?" I asked.

Olivia spun to face me and raised both her eyebrows with a hint of aggravation. I didn't know if she was going to shout at me for being rude or ridicule me. She did neither. Instead, she looked apprehensively over her shoulder, grabbed my waist and pulled me in close. As she softly pressed her lips against mine, I felt her form a smile. I broke away and whispered "Wh-what?"

She grinned and tucked a stray curl of mine behind my ear. "Nothing, you're just so silly and incredibly short-sighted!"

The next hour was spent sipping tentatively at a glass of rum and Coke Royston had poured for me. I wasn't particularly in the mood for drinking any more but the warmth of the alcohol certainly took the edge of the evening's surprises.

Tom was still as exuberant as ever, holding up the dance floor with his wayward two-step. After the lights came on to signal the end of the night, I thanked Royston again for his help.

"Don't let me catch you doing dat kind of nonsense again, ya hear me?" he scolded me.

I nodded and smiled wearily.

Olivia squeezed my hand and looked over at Tom, who was now slumped over a table with his glasses on his head.

Royston threw a tea towel over his shoulder. "Leave him here with me. I'll get him home. And, Olivia, you be careful. Ya hear me?"

I didn't know what Royston meant—as if I could have possibly been a bad influence on Olivia—but she replied, "I will," and swiftly took her hand away from mine.

We walked slowly and steadily to the taxi rank across the street. Thankfully there was a line of cars, so the wait wasn't long.

"What are you doing tomorrow?" I asked, with perhaps a little too much eagerness. I was never good at playing it cool especially not under the influence of alcohol.

Olivia hesitated for a moment, distracted by raised voices coming from a group of men in the queue. "Sorry, what did you say?"

"Tomorrow . . . do you have plans?" I asked again, trying harder this time not to sound too keen.

"I'm not sure yet. I have the day off but I should really do some research before the end of the week."

Was I really being blown off for homework?

"Okay, cool," I replied, disheartened but smiling all the same.

The taxi driver rolled down his window and asked me where I wanted to go.

"Bay View Inn, please."

He motioned for me to get into the back of car. Olivia hugged me and I took it as my opportunity to reciprocate her kiss. I leant in but she pulled away. I could almost taste the humiliation of the custard pie rolling down my face as we stood awkwardly on the pavement for a few seconds. The tension was finally broken when the taxi driver sucked his teeth and shouted, "Miss, you gettin' in?" I jumped at his voice and scrabbled for the door handle so I could climb in and hide my shame. As the car pulled away I could see Olivia waving in the rear-view mirror. I watched until the lights of the town faded into darkness.

My room was sweltering and I was certain the ceiling fan was just circulating hot air rather than cooling down the room. Pulling down my granny pants was one of the most satisfying events of the night. As I stepped out of the contraption I could almost hear my spongy middle squeal with delight as it escaped from under the boa constrictor waistband. I then tugged the dress down from my shoulders and onto the floor. My just-in-case outfit had done its job for the evening, encouraging disgusting perverts to leer over my cleavage. I knew there was a reason why I hated dresses.

I fell dramatically into bed and went over the comedy of errors from the evening. I was truly grateful that Royston found me, as things could have ended very badly. I knew how to circumnavigate threatening men, but under the influence of copious amounts of booze and wearing a dress that constricted my movement slashed the odds of me coming out on top.

And then there was Olivia who seemed so sweet and gentle. I couldn't quite figure her out. She was the one who initiated the kiss. She was the one who caught me off guard. She was the one who played with my giant frizzy hair. I had surmised that Olivia was just another girl who liked to kiss new friends and then casually bin them off at the end of a night. Oh, be still my beating heart, you incredibly attractive floozy! It was girls like her that made my coming out a disastrous homosexual awakening. I was inundated with ladies who wanted to use me as a crash-test dummy, before freaking out and protesting they were not gay. I hadn't kissed another girl since Liz, who I'm pretty sure exploited our three months of courtship and used it as a rehearsal for a role in a play that was axed after two nights. That was a year and a half ago. Maybe I was just a bad kisser. Maybe that's why Olivia wanted nothing more to do with me.

I rolled over like a distressed Disney princess who had been banished from the kingdom. I was unable to find a comfortable spot. My head was crammed with all sorts of cringe-filled nostalgia dating back to 1995. Self-flagellation was another one of my pastimes.

My gaze fell on Olivia's *Metanoia* book that lay on the floor next to the bed. I reached over to pick it up and then rolled onto my back. I opened the first page and began to read:

> Why did we stop believing in happily-ever-afters? Why did the magic of our imagination stop? Why did we settle instead of making the effort to change our mind, heart or way of life? Life can be amazing if we all stop overcomplicating the basic practice of gratitude. Being thankful for what we already have can and will magnetise deeper, positive and more satisfying outcomes and relationships in your life. You are the key to your transformation. Like attracts like.

I tried to suppress the instinctive eye rolling I often deployed when provoked with mumbo jumbo Kum ba yah spirituality. Mary had once suggested I speak to a doctor after my mother passed away, but I didn't feel sick so I couldn't understand why I should go. I stopped believing in happily-ever-afters after she died. My motto was "Life's a bitch and then you die", so New Age philosophy about appreciating the good in life seemed outrageous to me. When life excreted heartache over everything you loved, you just had to get on board. You suited up, grabbed a proton pack, and moved on, trying your best to handle the situation. I appreciated the fact that entertaining my sadness created a hotbed of contempt that bred further pain, but releasing the sludge of grief wasn't easy. Showing gratitude for my shitty life was not going to bring my mother back or stop my father dying.

My eyes began to sting with tears and I furiously rubbed them away. Stupid book.

Chapter Nineteen

The sunlight crept through the venetian blinds despite having closed them before bedtime. My bag from last night was still exactly where I had left it, lying on the woven bamboo mat after I had tossed it across the room like a bad-tempered child. I swung my body out of bed and hesitated. I wasn't entirely confident about which end the rum from last night would leave my body. Standing up quickly turned out to be a foolish move, so I immediately fell back onto the bed, praying I wouldn't vomit all over the sheets. With a few deep breaths, I rose again and hobbled to my bag to fetch my phone. The fact that the lack of signal was due to forces out of my control allowed me to relax in the knowledge that Mary couldn't be mad at me for not calling her back. The time across the screen read 8.35 a.m. It was ludicrously early for me and my hangover.

I climbed back into bed and stared at the ceiling fan. The rotating blades made my eyelids heavy. Maybe if I just stayed immobile, the urge to projectile vomit would pass. I closed my eyes and the image of Olivia unceremoniously dodging my affections barged to the forefront of my mind. On second thoughts, maybe I would just lie there and throw up, and then hopefully I would either choke on my own puke or lose all control of my bowel movements and die of further humiliation. I sounded as dramatic as Noah. I missed him. He would know what to do in this situation. Well, he would tell me to get a grip for starters and then encourage me to sign up for online dating again—a tried and tested process that had made me feel hideous. The only message I had received during a month's free trial was from a forty-seven-year-old man who invited me to have a threesome with him and his wife. I respectfully declined and then ate my feelings with a two-piece chicken meal from Mo's. At least Noah would have distracted me enough to stop the anxiety pangs reverberating in my stomach.

There was a crash outside my window as if someone had dropped a bag of spanners, and it jolted me out of my daydream. I slowly pulled a T-shirt over my head and tip-toed to the window. Snapping the blinds up, I looked down and saw the old man from the night I checked in. He was effortlessly carrying on his head a misshapen metal bucket filled with water. He saw me and waved, although his expression remained stony. I sceptically waved back with a look that said, "Why the hell do you have a bucket on your bloody head?" The old man walked past the abandoned pool and off through the gap in the bush, all the while perfectly balancing the bucket of water. I pushed the window open and breathed in the fresh air, hoping it would also purge the ill feelings circulating in my cesspit of a room. I could hear Effy singing from somewhere below and I figured, as I was already up, breakfast may be the only answer to the after-effects of rum and reggae.

A shower made me feel less like a genetically modified vegetable, but only just. There were no healing powers of euphoria gifted from the valley of Shangri-La this time, but washing my body somehow made me feel like less of a disaster. The fresh, soft water and pineapple-infused shower gel offered the illusion of normality, until I had to dress myself. Trying to clasp my bra proved to be a distressing situation. A simple, automatic routine I had been successfully doing since puberty was now far too challenging. I didn't think I was ever going to be one of those people who wore sunglasses inside, but at that moment I found daylight to be highly offensive. I stretched back onto my bed, sunglasses on, psyching myself up to move again. Lugging my sorry self down to Effy's kitchen felt like someone was repeatedly punching me in the face with every step I took. I tried my hardest to disguise my clouded state, but Effy clocked me straight away and screeched in delight at my misfortune.

"Oh, gurl, you really hit the rum punch hard last night, eh?"

I painfully nodded as she continued to cackle. I decided I didn't care what I ate as long as it came with a giant cup of tea or horse tranquilisers. Effy returned with a plate of hard-dough bread and a side helping of ackee and salted fish. I examined the dish from over my glasses, unsure of what exactly I was about to attempt to eat.

"Just try it! It will sort you out good and proper. Trust me!" Effy clapped her hands together and skipped back to the kitchen.

I edged my plastic chair closer to the table and poked my fork at the food. The ackee was yellow and jumbled with chopped green peppers, tomatoes and red onions. I decided to shovel a heap onto the bread and hope for the best. The taste was like nothing I had ever sampled.

The bread was deliciously dense and sweet, and the butter-coloured ackee had a similar texture and look to scrambled eggs, although it tasted absolutely nothing like eggs. The flakes of salted fish had a kick of peppery seasoning I knew I would never be able to replicate. Every morsel felt like angel dust flying down my throat. I wondered if it would taste this good if I puked it back up later. All that spice in the morning sun was making me sweat but I believed this to be a good thing if it was getting rid of the over-indulgence from my body.

Scraping my plate clean, I slowly sat back into the chair and sipped my tea. It was Tuesday and I had to get myself together for my trip to Georgetown. I wasn't there to have an adolescent tantrum about a girl I just met. Neither was I there to drink myself into a stupor.

My father's impending death gnawed away at the insides of my skull. I still had at least six weeks, if not more, to see him, but I also knew I didn't have time to divert from the plan. I would wait for my body to settle down from breakfast and then find that bus. But I had a feeling that such a straightforward plan wouldn't be so simple on an island that laughed in the face of efficiency.

Back at my room I switched on the TV and flicked through four static-filled news channels that all had a tinge of purple in the top right-hand corner of the screen. I finally found a music station that had no picture, just a blank screen churning out what I believed to be pirate radio.

I propped myself up against the headboard and looked at a map of the island I'd borrowed from reception. Georgetown was up the north-east coast from

Kingstown via the Windward Highway. I scanned the exotic names dotted across the creased paper, like Mesopotamia, Argyle and Calder, and then giggled at the sight of a town called Friendly. The French-sounding names such as Biabou, Barrouallie and Chateaubelair made me think that the laid-back simplicity of Vincentian life had a rich history I knew nothing about. I did, however, know all too well from my father's stories about the British colony, the horrors of slavery, and 'the crack of the master's whip.' But it was enunciating words such as "Baleine" and the volcano "La Soufrière" that made me crave more knowledge. I wanted to experience the island on my terms and not from the inside of a stuffy bus that would encourage my hangover to linger for the entire day. Effy was right—I needed to be a little adventurous. I needed to get that scooter.

Effy's cousin Leebut wheeled out a bright-orange scooter from his garage next to the B&B. The number plate had specks of rust and the paintwork, albeit eye-wateringly perky, had a fair few scratches. I was placing my life on the saddle of a limp-looking vehicle, but I grinned from ear-to-ear at the excitement of it all. Maybe I was still drunk.

"So, how much for the day? And what's the insurance policy?" I asked firmly in a faux middle-class accent, trying to conceal my enthusiasm and attempting to show that I was educated enough not be ripped off. Leebut scratched his patchy beard for a moment and then tilted his head.

"Gimme twenty dollar fi it . . . seeing as you friend with Effy!"

I had no idea if that was a good price or not, so haggling would have been pointless. "And the insurance?" I said as Leebut handed me a helmet.

"If you bruk it . . . you pay fi it!" And then he smiled with his hand out, ready to receive my money. I laughed nervously at the prospect of having to buy a brand-new scooter if I broke it, but I said nothing.

"'Ave you ever ride sumting like dis before?" Leebut asked with one eyebrow raised.

Not wanting to look stupid, I simply replied, "Why, yes of course!" as I swung my leg over the seat and stumbled to the side.

Leebut laughed out loud, knowing I was talking nonsense.

After patiently showing me the controls and a few practice runs up and down the large gravelled courtyard, I felt comfortable enough to go at it alone. I had my backpack over both shoulders, carrying all my essentials including a mango I bought from the market and my father's letter. I then tried my hardest to cram each wayward curl of my hair underneath the helmet. With a deep breath, I kicked the foot stand off the ground and began cautiously down the road towards town. I knew there was a sign for the Windward Highway from there, so that's where I would start. Leebut warned me that the roads could be interesting, whatever that meant, but it was the fastest most direct route to Georgetown. Flying past the sun-bleached fields either side of me, I felt euphoric, buzzing on a legal high of fresh air and sunshine. Although the engine spluttered every time I pushed the throttle, it still felt liberating to be doing something different. Clenching the metal frame between my thighs made me feel in control of at least one aspect of my life.

As I moved further down the road, I saw a figure in the distance. As I got close I recognised her and couldn't decide if I was happy or just vexed.

I pulled over to the grass verge and attempted to elegantly take my helmet off my trampled hair, but the buckle got caught.

Olivia giggled and tried to help me remove it.

"It's okay. I've got it!"

"Oh right, sorry," she mumbled, staring at the ground.

"What are you doing out this way?" I tried my best to regain some composure, but the pitch of my voice suggested I was trying too hard.

"I came to see you. I heard you tell the taxi driver the name of your hotel."

"It's not really a hotel," I said, and followed up with a fake laugh. I really needed to shut up.

"Well anyways, I wanted to . . . no, I needed to explain and apologise about last night."

"No, no, you don't have to explain anything!"

"No, I really do."

This was all very awkward. I dismounted the scooter and beckoned her to sit down at the side of the road. Nestled among overgrown weeds I began tugging at blades of grass and refused to hold eye contact with Olivia. I just wanted her to get on with the spiel.

"So I don't know if you know this, but St Vincent and the Caribbean in general are not too enthusiastic about . . . gays."

Not what I was expecting.

"Homosexuality is still illegal here, with the possibility of imprisonment for up to five years. And it's not just the law, it's also a bit of a cultural taboo. A few nights ago, a friend of Tom and mine was attacked outside a club in town. It took Royston and two other local men to drag the beast from him. Our friend ended up with a punctured lung and a fractured skull just because he mentioned he had a boyfriend back home."

I gasped and felt my breakfast move around in my stomach.

"We can probably get away with holding hands because we're girls and people are less offended with two females than two males for some idiotic reason, but anything else in public would be far too risky. That's why I was so weird at the end of the night. Not because I don't like you but because I was too frightened to be close to you."

I took a deep breath and leant forward as if someone had winded me. I was naïve to think that every country was as liberal as England. Thoughts of Noah rushed through my head, and although I missed him terribly, I was relieved he hadn't made this trip with me. He was far too unapologetically gay for the Caribbean.

"So that's why Royston told you to be careful when he saw you holding my hand?" I asked.

Olivia nodded. "Royston is one of the good guys, but he knows how small-minded some folk are. Don't get me wrong—I still love this place and so many of the locals. And not all Vincentians think this way. It's just a different culture, a different way of life, and we're just visitors. So, for now it's a case of discretion. Are you okay?"

I nodded but I didn't know what to say or even think. I hadn't fathomed concealing part of myself for the sake of being a law-abiding citizen, but here I was doing just that.

"Do you fancy a road trip?" I blurted out.

In truth, I wasn't sure if I wanted Olivia to come with me. I wasn't even sure if I wanted anyone to be around me when I visited my father's favourite place, but it was too late now.

Chapter Twenty

O livia hopped onto the back of the bike and wrapped her arms around my waist. It might have looked like a romantic scene from a movie, but the situation was far from dreamy. Any intentions of a holiday romance were thwarted by the prospect of being gay-bashed by homophobic hooligans. Having Olivia so close should have willed parts of my body to flutter uncontrollably, but instead it scared the hell out of me. Having an extra person on the scooter also made balancing a lot trickier on corners, but my real nerves came from feeling like a giant dyke on a bike. I felt like we were Sims computer game characters with a giant LGBT rainbow hovering above our heads and a sign that read, "Honk if you hate lesbians!"

Since coming out I had never had to check my sexuality. I lived in one of the most liberal, freethinking cities in the world. If you didn't tick an 'ethnic other' box on a doctor's form, or had yet to embark on a journey of sexual discovery in the queue for the toilets in a Soho bar, then you weren't doing London right. I'd never had to be wary of being "too gay" for fear of persecution. The thoughts of complete strangers resorting to violence over my sexual preference made me feel sick. Twenty minutes into the journey, and further into the countryside, we made a pit stop along a quiet path from the main road, to drink a bottle of warm water and share my soft, dented mango.

"So, are you going to tell me why we're going to Georgetown?" Olivia asked dubiously.

"I just want to see if I can find my dad's old house, take a photo and tick it off the to-do list!" I smiled nervously. My smile was transparent but I didn't think Olivia was brave enough to question my real motives just yet.

Back on the scooter, we headed further up the coast on uneven road cut out of the rock that gave way to a sheer drop into the sea. I tried my hardest to ignore the crashing waves and the signs alerting us to falling rocks as I began reciting my third Hail Mary. We also witnessed some of the maniacal drivers who clearly had suicidal tendencies. Turning one sharp corner, I was confronted with a truck whose driver believed both sides of the road belonged to him. I swerved just in time and felt Olivia's grip tighten around my waist. As we safely passed the truck, I instinctively reached for her hand to make sure she was okay. She rested her head onto my back and kept it there until we stopped at the village of Friendly.

The brightly coloured colonial-looking houses were pretty. The village was like a supersized painter's palette, with shades of pastel yellow brickwork, pink rooftops, bright-blue fences and purple facades, all surrounded by lush green plants and trees. Even the intricate verandahs were beautiful. I parked the bike outside of what looked like a convenience store and went in search of chilled water. Wearing a helmet in the heat was draining and sweaty. I needed to douse myself in cold water and shake off the uncomfortable sensation of sweat sliding down my back.

"Excuse me, is Georgetown nearby?" I said to the old lady behind the counter. She was wearing a tabard and sat on a crate of glass Sprite bottles. Her legs were stretched wide underneath her long skirt, as she fanned herself with what looked like the plastic lid from a Tupperware box.

The old lady stopped fanning, looked me up and down and smiled. She was completely toothless. She then reached into her pocket and pulled out a set of dentures. With one swift movement and a jiggle of her jaw, she began to speak.

"Oh yes, darlin'! If you wan' Georgetown, just look it over dere so . . . no more than five minutes up da road!"

I nodded and smiled, almost mesmerised at her ability to not care about what others might think of her dental situation. I handed over the money for the bottle of water, chuckled to myself and left.

"Do you fancy taking a little stroll?" Olivia asked wide-eyed and eager to explore. I folded the map into my bag and fiddled with my hair. We walked in the direction of the only tarmacked road we could see, heading downhill into thick vegetation, with grass up to my knee. Olivia took out her camera and started snapping away at the wildlife. She was edging farther and farther into the bushes, and I hesitated, swatting a fly away from my face, unsure if we would be attacked by a wild animal. She turned around and laughed at my obvious apprehension.

"Come on, scaredy, I'll protect you!" She held out her hand to hold and I followed her in.

"You do realise we are now starring in our own slasher film! Think *The Blair Witch Project* meets *Buffy the Vampire Slayer*!" I said. I cleared my throat and improvised a horror-movie trailer voiceover: "Two idiotic girls decide to head into the unknown and encounter mutated cannibals with a thirst for human flesh! The pretty blonde just wanted an adventure. Her companion, the wiser, token lady of colour with ginormous hair insisted it was a bad idea. But instead of listening to her gut, she followed her vagina!"

We both laughed and it felt good. It was the first time that day I felt at ease.

"So, urm . . . you think I'm pretty?" Olivia teased walking slowly towards me with the same daring look from the night before.

"Well . . . I mean . . . sure . . . you're okay!"

Then she kissed me.

This time it was deeper and cut with more passion. She touched the side of my clammy cheek and I twitched uneasily at her having to get so close to my sweaty, freckled face.

She withdrew and breathed, "Stop! I like your sticky skin!" and then she softly kissed my cheek. I accidentally dropped my helmet on the ground and for the first time in so long, I felt like I had dropped my guard.

A few more photographs later, it was time to leave the tiny town of Friendly. As we emerged from the canopy of huge banana leaves, I remembered to leave my lust in the forest. I wasn't willing to test just how friendly the town was when it came to public displays of affection. A few locals waved, a disorientated goat attempted to cross the road and an old man tipped his hat and said good afternoon as we settled back on the scooter. Georgetown was only a short drive away, and for the first time since arriving in St Vincent, my stomach flipped at the enormity of finally being there.

Dodging between various open-top vehicles and a man pushing a wheelbarrow full of logs, we finally whizzed through a small tunnel and entered Georgetown. The town was buzzing with people and barefooted children playing at the side of the road. There were banks, large supermarkets and other office buildings. Teenage girls were talking animatedly on their smartphones. Heads turned as I parked outside a busy-looking supermarket. I didn't know if it was the orange bike drawing attention or the fact that not many tourists made it that far into the island. The staring unnerved me and I dropped the scooter keys.

"Maya, stop worrying and breathe!" Olivia said.

I exhaled long and slowly. I did need to stop worrying. I adjusted my sunglasses. I also needed to eat.

Across from the supermarket there was a small café with a handwritten sign outside listing the daily specials. I pulled the door open and smiled at the young slim girl near the till. She gestured for us to take a seat and so I sat down with a satisfying sigh. Scanning the menu, I was determined to try something new again. I wanted to continue my education in Caribbean food by ordering a dish I had never heard of before.

"What is a roti?" I asked Olivia hoping she could shed some light.

"Oh, you'll love it!" she replied enthusiastically.

The waitress came over and Olivia ordered two chicken rotis and a drink called Red Ju-C. I leant back in my chair and massaged the back of my neck. Olivia nervously shifted in her seat and then sheepishly said, "So, are you going to tell me why we're really here?"

Chapter Twenty-One

Olivia listened as I explained how my dad was lying in a hospital bed somewhere in New York, dying of cancer. Saying the words out loud sounded so ludicrously dramatic that I almost wanted to laugh. It sounded like it wasn't happening to me but instead was a scene from one of my soap operas. Despite feeling I was beginning to trust Olivia, I didn't elaborate on the relationship I had with my dad. I told her I wanted to see the place he loved the most and attempt to retrieve his boyhood treasure. Olivia went to reach for my hand as the waitress clattered our order onto the table. "Enjoy, ladies!" The waitress chimed sweetly, breaking the weird tension.

I carefully swivelled the plate, observing the roti from all angles, and my mouth filled with saliva. "This looks amazing!" I grabbed the knife and fork and attacked the chunks of saffron-curried chicken oozing out of what appeared to be a flatbread. I wanted to bathe in the spicy sauce. I was certain I would return to the UK twelve stone heavier, but I wouldn't be sorry.

"Try some of the Ju-C!" Olivia pushed the large glass bottle closer to me. "It's a Vincy national treasure!"

The red liquid was like Cherryade but included at least five more tablespoons of sugar and possibly some kind of opiate. The sweet bubbles fizzed up my nose as I coughed all over my lunch.

"Maybe I'll just stick to water!" I spluttered.

The next twenty minutes were whiled away talking about Caribbean dishes, from curry goat, rice and peas to jerk chicken and fried breadfruit. I was game to try all of those and more.

We chatted about Olivia's holiday in Barbados and the tattoo she planned to get in town. Then she suddenly said, "Maya, I shouldn't have come here with you."

I blinked and tilted my head, unsure of what she meant. I invited her, so of course on some level I wanted her with me. If this was another brush off, I didn't think my patience could handle it again.

"What do you mean?" My eyes narrowed.

Olivia understood exactly what I was thinking. "No, no," she said, "I don't mean I regret coming. I just think this daytrip was something you needed to do on your own."

I rubbed the side of my head, frustrated from not knowing what the hell I was doing or even wanted. Perhaps she was right.

I finally muttered, "I don't know."

Olivia reached for my hand again.

"I can come with you if you want."

I closed my eyes and rubbed my chest. It wasn't heartburn; I just wanted to be sure my heart was still doing its job.

"Maybe you're right. This should be something I do by myself, but the truth is I don't think I would have made it this far. I wanted to turn back as soon as we left Kingstown and the only reason I kept pushing the throttle of that bloody bike was because I didn't feel like I was on my own."

"Okay, right, it's settled." Olivia called the waitress over so we could pay the bill. "Do you have an address or any clue as to where your dad's old house is?"

I removed his letter from the side pocket of my bag and read over the words. "All I know from what he told me years ago was that they lived over the bridge on Caratal River and in the letter he mentions a neighbour called Mr Benjamin."

The waitress immediately stopped what she was doing. "You mean Arnold Benjamin?" she asked curiously. I shrugged and scanned the letter to see if there was any mention of Mr Benjamin's first name.

"Well dere was only one Benjamin by da river and dat was me h'uncle. He passed some years ago now but him house is still dere. I don' know nutin' bout da neighbours but look . . . da address 'ere." The waitress wrote on the back of the receipt and handed me the piece of paper with a wink.

"Just follow da road roun' to da river and keep left. You carn' miss it." And with a broad encouraging smile, she turned and headed to the kitchen.

Back on the scooter I felt invigorated once again. It was like a TV challenge game from the early 1990s, where the sole purpose of the game was to watch a breathless lady in a tracksuit running around with rubbish clues, a headset and a confused camera crew. There were a few beeps of horns and "Hey, girls" from overconfident gentleman, but this time it didn't bother me. I was too preoccupied with finding the hidden treasure and celebrating with a can of Red Stripe. My hangover was a thing of the past as the cool breeze whipped across my face and we turned down the street towards the river.

After about five minutes I saw children ahead, running over a dip in the grassy bank towards the side of running water. I knew we were close. Olivia tapped me on the back and pointed out to the scenery to the left. There were tall overlapping hills in various shades of green. Trees looped over boulders, birds dived and streams seemed to stretch out for miles. It was breathtaking. We came to a fork in the road and kept left. We then arrived at an unkempt green with four crumbling houses leaning precariously against each other. I turned off the engine and felt my heart drop at the sight that lay before me.

What may have once been a close-knit neighbourhood was now a dumpsite only fit for demolition. This couldn't be it. I looked at the receipt with the address on as if I had missed something. Number 3, Caratal Riverside. Walking amid the debris the river had thrown up, I felt a sense of sadness. It looked like a flood had destroyed nearly everything. The waitress was correct when she said Mr Benjamin's house was still there, but only just. I could see the rusted number three hanging lopsided on what remained of the front door. Part of the verandah was missing, and even the outside latrine had disintegrated into a pile of broken wood and corrugated iron. My father's old house next door was just as bad. Suddenly there was a loud crash inside the apparently abandoned building. Olivia and I gasped at the frightful noise.

"Hello?" I called. There was only silence, and I began to step away just as a stray dog came hurtling out and ran off into the distance.

With a deep sigh of relief, I looked over my shoulder to Olivia, who smiled. I faced once again the home of my father and realised there was not one banana tree on the land. I would never find his beloved toy car.

"Are you okay?" Olivia was now standing beside me.

"Yeah, I'm fine," I lied. I then reached into my bag for my camera.

"I'm just going to take a few photos. I won't be a minute." I smiled even though I was far from happy.

Olivia placed her hand gently on my shoulder and said she would wait by the scooter. I kicked an empty Pepsi can in annoyance. I felt crestfallen, like the entire trip was a pointless exercise. But then again maybe it was a sign. A sign to tell me to leave all my shit in the past and just move on.

I snapped away at the scene all the same. At least I could take away some family history, even if I'd never really known the family. I found a long knobbly stick and used it to prod the muddy ground in frustration. I walked through what I imagined was my father's front garden and stood there for a moment with my eyes closed.

In the kitchen stands my grandmother baking bread and stirring a pot of something mouth-watering for dinner. She's just shouted out to Auntie Lou Lou who is playing with her dolls in the front room, to help her lay the table. With a sassy eye roll, she reluctantly hurries to the kitchen, knowing not to test my grandmother's patience. My father is playing with his car on the front porch. He's making the engine noises as he runs the tiny wheels of his toy across the uneven grass. He looks so happy. He has the same smile on his face he used to have when he danced with my mother in the kitchen.

I opened my eyes and stepped back. With one last click of my camera, I turned to leave. My foot caught on something hard and solid in the ground and I stumbled, cursing the earth. Hopping painfully from stubbing my toe, I steadied myself trying to furiously unearth whatever did me the injury. I stooped closer to the ground, narrowing my eyes. With the palm of my hand I wiped away the grey sand to reveal a tree stump. My eyes widened. It was the base of a tree that had obviously been cut down some time ago.

My head was unable to process what came next. It was like there was a three-second lag with my brain as it failed to keep up with the speed of my hands. I began ripping into the soil beneath my feet using my stick as a makeshift spade. I reached deeper and deeper into the earth, persevering like a woman possessed. I dabbed away what I thought was sweat but was in fact tears streaming down my face. With one last dive into the ground, I felt something solid. I moved away a lump of soil and revealed a tiny wheel. I made sure not to force it out for fear of breaking it, so I softly wiggled it until finally I was face to face with a small yellow toy car. I slowly turned it over and wiped away the dirt. Engraved into the base of the car were the initials C.T.

Chapter Twenty-Two

Once I had it in my hand, I didn't want to let it go. Not even when Olivia sat down next to me and I cried uncontrollably for twenty minutes straight.

"I'm going to have to enter witness protection and hide from all of the humiliation after today," I said, forcing a smile. "Come on a road trip, I said. It'll be fun, I said. Well that was a rubbish idea!"

Olivia smiled, jabbed me in the side and brushed away a tear from my cheek. "I think today was the best idea! You found what you were looking for!"

I stared at the small Matchbox car in the palm of my dirty hand. I wanted to feel jubilant but something didn't feel right. I feared I had opened Pandora's box.

"I think I'm a little bit fucked." I dropped my head as if the weight of it was too much to keep upright.

"Then unfuck yourself! Be the person you want to be and do the things you want to do before whatever your dad did breaks you beyond all repair. Read the bloody book. It's not all hippy dippy crap!"

I chuckled. It was extraordinary to have Olivia splash around in my murky puddle of dysfunction.

The girl made sense, but it was easier said than done. Nobody had prepared me for life continually dumping distressing situations on my head from a great height. I was trying to learn to suck it up and move on. But staring at the toy, I wasn't sure if I could. There was still a part of me aching from the upset of my father. The only thing that became clear now was that I needed to see him. I had questions that needed to be answered. I began to pace back and forth trying to shake off the emotions I was feeling. I felt a wave of anger. The burning hatred I felt towards my father every time he pummelled my mother across a room was back with a vengeance. I tucked the toy car into the side of my bag. Out of sight, out of mind.

I wheeled the scooter to the side of the road and led the way on foot towards the bustle of a road and past a secondary school with walls that were painted mint green. We walked in silence as I took in more brightly coloured colonial houses. Schoolchildren waved at us and then quickly ran away giggling at the two strange tourists.

Olivia and I continued to follow the main road that was lined with electricity poles. The electric wires twisted wildly above our heads running through the giant branches of coconut trees that grew in people's gardens. We veered around a corner, and as I stooped to take a photograph of a barefoot teenage boy playing keepy uppy with a football, I heard voices singing. I looked at Olivia and then turned to face the sound. It was coming from a Baptist church on the corner of the road.

"Do you fancy going in?" I asked, surprising myself with the question. I hadn't been in a church since my mother died, but the hum of music was strangely enticing. Olivia held out her hand and we both walked towards the sound.

I always expected silence and grandeur in churches, but this one was different. There was no ornate altar or fancy stained glass, and no sign of bronze or gold religious motifs. Instead, the four bare stone walls were decorated with children's arts and crafts and there was a modest wooden cross behind the altar. Children filled the timeworn pews as they had, no doubt, for generations.

A tall gentleman standing at the side of an aisle spotted Olivia and me and, with a welcoming grin, motioned us to take a seat. We shuffled discretely into the pews at the back, not wanting to interrupt what appeared to be choir rehearsal.

I had never witnessed so many young people genuinely excited to be at church singing hymns. Every Thursday morning at my school, the reverend would conduct an assembly and we were forced to sing about Jesus being our best friend. And every Thursday morning without fail there was an audible groan as the Rev would try to deliver a sermon to a bunch of bored teenagers whose only interest was clock-watching until the final bell. Looking at the faces of the children here, it appeared they were having the time of their lives. The energy was palpable as hands clapped, tambourines were shaken, the organ bellowed and the choirmaster encouraged the performance with his James Brown-inspired moves.

The choirmaster turned around to the new faces and urged us to stand and join in a traditional call-and-response gospel song. Olivia and I looked awkwardly at each other, trying not to laugh out of embarrassment, but as the song progressed, I realised I had heard it before. It was a hymn my father would sometimes sing when he was shaving in the bathroom. Half of his face would be covered in shaving foam as he would pop his head around the door so I could sing along with him while he waved his razor in the air like a conductor's baton. He would start the first line of the chorus and I would answer him.

"Maya, how do you feel?"

"I feel alriiiiight!"

"I said, Maya, how do you feel?"

"I feel alriiiiight . . . for there's no condemnation in my soul."

The lyrics jolted me out of my seat and I was now standing with the rest of them, clapping enthusiastically like a TV evangelist. I felt a strange sense of empowerment as if I was immersed in a throng of old negro spirituals communicating my oppression in a safe environment. It was only as Olivia placed her hand on the small of my back that I felt the teardrop on my cheek.

After some well-deserved applause, we decided to duck out and head back outside. My heart continued to pound with excitement.

"That was epic!" Olivia shrieked. "I would happily be a born-again Christian if mass with Father Laurence on a Sunday was that entertaining!"

I grinned at the sudden leap in both of our spirits. For a moment, it made me forget my deep feelings of sadness. I did however feel it was time to leave Georgetown and make our way back.

As we neared the scooter, Olivia held out her hand. "Keys. You're not driving. Your unbalanced mojo may just get us killed! Well, that's if a Vincy driver doesn't kill us first!"

She made me smile and I wanted to kiss her, but it was the middle of the day on a busy street. I placed the keys to the scooter in her hand and adjusted myself on the back of the bike.

"Are you sure you're okay with driving?" I asked, slightly nervous.

"Just hang on and I guess we'll find out!" Olivia replied, revving the engine as if the tiny satsuma of a bike were a Harley.

Sitting on the back of the scooter was a whole new experience. I could take in the world around me without thinking I was playing chicken with the devil. The danger of falling off a cliff or being involved in a head-on collision with a truck felt bizarrely exciting now I wasn't in control. Olivia was a great driver anyway, better than me. People waved from the side of the road and I waved back. I felt a new sense of freedom and relinquished my bad vibes to the cool Vincentian breeze. I also loved being physically close to Olivia without the worry of causing an accident. My mind relaxed and I rested the side of my head on Olivia's shoulder.

Chapter Twenty-Three

We finally arrived back in Kingstown in the late afternoon after two near misses with an overcrowded truck of fruit and a complete tosser in a jeep. Olivia parked up outside Royston's bar, and I had never been so happy to drink so soon after a debauched night of alcohol abuse. I was calmer but my head was still jam-packed with thoughts of my father. Olivia ordered us each a rum and Coke and I played with the menu on the table. As she sat down, Olivia was trying, unsuccessfully, to restrain her laughter.

"Maya, my darling, your hair is a vision!"

I frantically tried to flatten my windswept locks but finally just shrugged and stuck out my tongue. I took a few large gulps of my drink and was instantly transported back to last night. I closed my eyes at the kick from the rum and then refocused.

"So, do you want to talk about it . . . or will we just continue ignoring the giant elephant in the room wearing a belly top and stilettos?" Olivia asked, tilting her head to try to lock eyes with me. There was something fantastically reassuring about being around her. Even though I had just met her, she made me feel I was capable of picking up the broken parts of my life and Sellotaping them back together. Yet the idea of letting her in absolutely terrified me.

"For now I'd prefer to sit back and admire the awkwardness of the belly-top-wearing elephant in the corner. Maybe we can talk another time." I smiled and

Olivia nodded. I knew I would have to decipher the crazies in my head at some point, but I just hadn't reached that point quite yet. I simply wanted to sit with being emotionally unavailable for a little bit longer.

I carefully placed my empty glass on the table and told Olivia I was going to head back to the B&B and return the scooter. It had already been such a long day. She asked if I wanted company but I declined. I already felt like I had kidnapped her into a weird day trip that was essentially just me being an emotional mess. Plus, I longed for some alone time without having to be aware of myself in front of someone I quite liked.

"There's an all-day beach party on the island of Bequia tomorrow," Olivia said as we left the bar. "We're getting the boat over at 11 a.m. You should totally come . . . that's if, um, you'd like to?"

"That sounds great!" I replied. "I haven't even been to the beach yet, so it would be perfect!"

Olivia's smile spread across her face once again. We both hesitated to embrace each other. I'm sure we were being overcautious now but it was becoming a bad habit we couldn't break.

"I'll see you tomorrow then," Olivia muttered, staring coyly at the ground. And then, in an act of spontaneity, she gave me a quick peck on the lips and skipped off towards the port.

Although I had always hoped someone would like me more than just as a friend, in all my imperfect glory, I was equally petrified of falling in love. I believed that love brought immeasurable pain and chaos. Once you had it, you opened yourself up to all manner of heartbreak. Love for me had always been like pain, and I needed to protect what remained of the squishy thing in the left-hand side of my chest. I wasn't so naïve as to think that after two days I had found 'the one', but I had never felt so strongly drawn to someone who wasn't a fictional TV character or the lady in the Vitabiotics Wellwoman advert on the Tube. As I watched Olivia leave I realised that, astonishingly, this was someone who seemed to like me and I didn't know what to do with that information, or the butterflies that were having an illegal rave in the pit of my stomach.

I pulled up outside Leebut's garage and I could hear a radio inside the garage playing "Monkey Man" by Toots and the Maytals. The chorus kicked in and my insides jumped. The song sent me right back to car journeys with my dad, me sitting in the back seat counting telephone poles and him tapping the steering wheel with his hands as if it were a drum. Music was a time machine. It had the power to pick me up like a claw machine at a seaside arcade and then drop me down in a memory I thought I had lost. I had always loved this song.

After a few minutes of calling out to Leebut with no luck, I pushed the scooter up to the back door of the garage and hung the helmet on the handlebars. I then took a piece of paper from my bag and scrawled: "Thank you for the little adventure!" and tucked it behind the headlight.

I strolled slowly back to the B&B, kicking at loose stones and watching the clouds move above me. Everything was reminding me of him. I hadn't expected the island to conjure up such vivid memories of my father. I didn't want to lose a grip of the hatred I held for him, but with each day it was becoming progressively harder, when I was falling in love with St Vincent—the chat of the locals, the food, the music, the light.

I turned my head to the sky again and looked at the trees stretching upward, like gnarled giants trying to shake hands with the sun. The clouds were soaked in an amber glow and I thought of my mother. I wondered what she would think of my recent escapades. She always encouraged the bond between me and my father, even when I refused to speak to him after another abusive incident. "He's your father, Maya, and he loves you."

I had no appetite, so I headed straight to my room. The bed had been made again and my suitcase was tidied away, so it didn't look like the remnants of an explosive jumble sale. I placed the toy car on the bed along with the letter from my dad. I then retrieved the photograph of my mother and I rested it next to the other items. Sitting cross-legged on the bed, I examined the objects, hoping I could make sense of why I felt so utterly miserable, and then I realised this was all I had left of my parents. The letter, photo and toy car were the only physical objects I had to show for a dead mother and a dying, estranged father. I didn't know how to articulate the feeling of loss, anger and the choking of sadness. It was all too intense, and my eyes were too raw to cry again.

I delved into my bag for my iPod and slipped my headphones on. Maybe I didn't need to put words to my emotions. Maybe I could just tumble into a musical coma of show tunes, power ballads and Lovers' rock. I hoped a lyric from a song would put me back together before I fell apart again. I lay watching the slow rotation of the ceiling fan and placed all my anxiety into the music. The songs expressed what I couldn't and it soothed me. Maybe tomorrow I would try to unfuck myself as Olivia had so eloquently suggested, but right then I just wanted to close my eyes and play pretend.

Chapter Twenty-Four

It was 2005. The year Prince Charles and Camilla tied the knot, James Blunt crooned to millions about how beautiful they were, and the terrorist attacks in London tore through everyone's belief that "It will never happen to me." As the news channel pumped out blow-by-blow updates, Aileen sat forward in her armchair and watched the frantic emergency services and weeping bystanders with bloodied faces. She held her breath as her eyes glistened and her heart broke for fifty-two innocent strangers.

It always takes a horrendous event to remind us that life is fragile and that at any moment loved ones could be permanently snatched away. Aileen raised herself from the armchair with a deep sigh. It was an exhalation of breath that conveyed a sadness to the smack of life that she had been wrestling with for years.

She stared into the large mirror in the hallway and used the tips of her fingers to push and pull the translucent skin of her face over her angular bone structure. The freckles were still as prominent as ever, but the deep shadows underneath her eyes made her face look more skeletal than before. Her disappointment with life hung from every crease and fold in her sunken flesh. She ran her fingers through her auburn hair that had lost its sheen and settled unenthusiastically on her shoulders. She then swept a strand of hair behind her ear and grimaced at the latest bruise.

It was the middle of the day and she had one precious hour to herself before her daughter arrived back from school. It was that hour of the day when Aileen could sit by herself to summon another gear of resilience to get through the evening with as little drama as possible. She sat on the bottom step of the stairs and hugged her knees into her chest. She had become the person she vowed she would never become. The idea of being subservient to a man who dominated her with mental and physical pain, was everything she had strived to avoid. She had watched her father hurl abuse at her own mother, when she was just a child, and now Aileen was perpetuating that nightmare. The rebellious will to live by her own rules and never bend to a man had diminished with every clout, and with the responsibility of protecting her daughter.

The man she loved was still there. He had to be. Work was tough and money was far from abundant. Those factors alone would cause trouble for a couple. "Surely," Aileen muttered aloud to herself as she rationalised her situation yet again. Sometimes, when he was in a good mood, she would see the man she married. The man she left her home and family for to start the life she craved so desperately. The kindness was still buried deep within Cedric's eyes every time his favourite song came on the radio or each time he twirled her in an impromptu dance routine in the kitchen, and it was that look that made her forgive him again and again.

Aileen missed her family—She couldn't help it—and listening to the accounts of grief-stricken family members of the victims of the London bombings made her yearn for the safety of her *Under Milk Wood* lifestyle once again, where bugger all occurred and nobody tried to escape from the clan in an attempt to forge a better life for themselves.

"You can't leave!" Aileen's sister protested on the evening she was packing her bag.

Aileen paused as her chest fluttered with sadness.

"You can't leave . . . me," her sister croaked through the tears.

Aileen swept up her belongings, planted a kiss on her sister's cheek and exited her old life through the bedroom window under which Cedric was waiting. Although the sisters shared hushed phone conversations during stolen moments over the years, it was never the same or would be the same again. Her heart broke every time her sister said, "I love you" and she would reply, "I love you too."

There were times when Aileen would dial the number of her parents' house, panic at the prospect of hearing her mother or father's voice and then immediately hang up before anyone had a chance to answer. Although she loathed the suffocation and lack of imagination of her hometown, she still missed it terribly. In the moments when she dabbed the blood from her burst bottom lip, she often wished her father had tried harder to end her relationship with Cedric. She would replay the shouldas, couldas and wouldas of the night Cedric was beaten within an inch of his life and left for dead at the bus stop, and then picture her life without him. If only they had stomped on his head just one more time. If only the cricket bat her father had used was struck with more force against Cedric's skull. If only she had never decided to intervene and offer him that haircut. But then the pang of disgust and guilt for the man she couldn't help but love would drag her out of her thoughts of escape.

Aileen didn't want to make the same mistake with her own family. No matter how dysfunctional the Thomases were, she still didn't want her daughter living the same stifled lifestyle that was inflicted upon her. Aileen owed it to herself and her daughter to keep it together, despite her impulse to flee into the night and never return. She wanted her daughter to grow up with the same principles of self-reliance and independence she once had. She wanted her daughter to be stronger than she had been and not let love complicate her life. Aileen more than anything wanted to teach her daughter that sometimes love was simply not enough, and forgiveness can take time.

Aileen heaved herself upright with the help of the chipped bannister. She slowly walked into the kitchen and began putting pots and pans on the breakfast bar in preparation for dinner. Her movements were automatic, with a heavy air of monotony and boredom. As she wrapped the string of her apron around her petite waist, the front door rattled with the sound of a key wriggling its way into the lock. The latch clicked and Aileen held her breath and swallowed hard. In bounded her daughter and Aileen's heart rose and flickered with relief.

"Maya, darling, how do you fancy a trip to London in a few weeks, for your birthday? We can go for the day, watch a musical and you can eat whatever you like!"

Maya looked at her mother with scepticism and narrowed eyes that were questioning her sudden brightness. She burst into a smile that had been missing from her face for weeks and replied, "That sounds amazing! Is Dad coming?" She lowered her voice at the mention of her father.

"No, no, this will be our trip. Just you and me in the big city. You need to get out and see more of the world beyond this awful council estate. And we need to show these wicked individuals on the news that we're not afraid."

Before Aileen had finished her sentence, her daughter was beside her hugging the side of her waist and resting her head on her shoulder. Aileen's body eased into her daughter's embrace and she kissed the wild caramel curls on top of her head.

"Now go get yourself ready for dinner. Your father will be home soon."

Chapter Twenty-Five

I t was nice to wake up the following morning without feeling like my head had been tenderised with a meat mallet. I was able to get from my bed to the bathroom without feeling obliterated by jetlag or poor life choices involving rum. Looking at myself in the mirror always proved a struggle in the morning but today I didn't mind. Yes, my hair was now double the size and resembled a five-year-old's art project. And yes, my face was now one big cluster of freckles, but there was a certain healthy shimmer to my skin. I observed myself from all angles, impressed I had strap marks from the top I had worn the day before. As I stepped into the shower I was committed to having a great day despite yesterday's discovery and the feelings it dredged up. It was my last full day in St Vincent and I intended to spend it having fun.

I decided I would grab some breakfast in town on the way down to the boat that morning. I was craving fresh mango and pineapple, which was a far cry from the Kit Kat I would unashamedly chow down on during my morning commute to work. So, with my hair tied back and my sunglasses on, I stepped into the scorching morning sun with my giant beach bag for company and the sound of my flip-flops slapping up and down on the dusty pathway. With every "Psst, hey gal!" I received from passing men, who Effy said had "no shame fi dem eye!" I simply added an extra bounce to my walk. If my rotund arse bobbing freely inside my shorts drew attention, then screw it. I was on my holidays!

Turning into the street wedged tightly with market stalls, I made a beeline for the fruit. The lady recognised me from before and she kindly sliced up some juicy melon for me to eat while she packed a bag with the rest of my fruit. Today she was wearing a flamboyant blonde wig that was aggravating her in the hot sun. I watched her lift part of the fringe at the front and scratch her forehead. She caught my eye and spoke.

"Eh, eh, gyal, you looking good! Me see a lickle piece of sun has catch your backside!" She cackled loudly at her own joke as I tried to check out my rear end.

A deep voice spoke from behind me. "She just means you've got a tan." It was Royston. He was still unshaven but his shirt wasn't as revealing as it was from the previous night.

"Oh . . . right . . . yes! I know!" I didn't know at all.

The lady handed me my bag of fruit with a wink.

"So what brings you here?" I asked.

"I'm just buying a few bits. It's going to be a busy night for me after the beach party so I'm stocking up." He appeared agitated as ever, as if everyone was stalling him from getting on with his day.

"Oh right, yes. I'm off to meet Olivia now. It sounds like it's going to be fun!" I tried to inject some enthusiasm into the conversation.

"Okay, cool," Royston replied aloofly, and then raised his hand to get someone's attention from behind me.

"Well, I should go!" I waved goodbye and walked away convinced I would never be able to crack the enigma of Royston.

As I headed down the boardwalk to the port I felt a little uneasy. Knowing that strange men intimidated young women there was not a nice feeling. The setup was much different that morning, however. There were lots of bodies busying around and so it made no sense to feel frightened in the daylight. My heart rate kept racing, though. I was distracted from my apprehension by a young busker playing a steel pan drum at the side of the path. The short sticks in his hands moved gracefully over the dented tin to a melody that sounded like the soundtrack of island life. I threw a few coins into his bucket and he smiled with a face that oozed genuine warmth and gratitude. I had no idea where I was to meet Olivia but I was sure I would see her as I waited close to a group of people talking about Bequia. I perched on the side of a low wall and took out my phone. It was 10.45 and I still had no signal but I was over the feeling of being cut off from modernity. I looked up but I couldn't spot Olivia so I indulged in a game of Snake on my phone. It didn't take me long to get frustrated at dying prematurely and I muttered "Stupid arsing game!" under my breath before throwing the phone back in my bag.

I looked up again. Olivia, Tom, and another girl I didn't recognise were striding over in my direction. I stood up and waved and then felt my cheeks smart with red when Olivia saw me and waved back. It felt so strange to have such an overwhelming reaction. Olivia came closer for an innocent peck on the cheek and Tom followed suit.

"The last time I saw you, you were sprawled over a table after an epic night of dancing the robot!" I teased him.

He shook his head and face-palmed. "Yeah, Royston had to bring me home! I spent the entire next day in bed hating my life!" He laughed at himself.

There was an intentional cough from behind him as the unfamiliar girl stepped out into full view.

"Ah yes, this is Ruby." Olivia was noticeably unenthusiastic. "She also works with Tom and me so she figured she would come along today."

Ruby was wearing a sarong and a skimpy bikini that displayed two perfectly pert breasts. She looked like she belonged on the front cover of a lads' mag. She then peered over her large sunglasses and offered her limp hand and waited for me to shake it, or kiss it, and then perhaps curtsy. She instantly struck me as someone who knew exactly just how attractive she was. I had to focus. I needed to maintain eye contact.

"Nice to meet you, Ruby. I'm Maya." I shook her hand far too vigorously.

"Olivia invited me, so of course I was going to come!" Ruby's voice was irritatingly nasal.

Tom and Ruby walked ahead down the pier and I had a chance to catch Olivia on her own. "You look nice!" I whispered, and for the first time I saw Olivia flush with embarrassment.

"Likewise," she replied with a meek smile, playing with her chunky beaded necklace, as if she was momentarily stunned from losing her much-preferred role of being in control of her emotions.

"So what's the deal with Ruby?" I asked, raising both eyebrows.

Olivia sighed deeply and checked to see if we were being overheard. "She just invited herself! Tom and I were getting ready to leave and then next of all she's coming with us. I didn't know what to say. I mean she's generally okay, but what she believes is confidence can come across as unadulterated arrogance. I'm hoping Tom babysits her for most of the day."

I gave her a smile and relaxed somewhat in the knowledge that Olivia didn't reciprocate Ruby's keenness.

"Maya . . . yesterday . . . I really think . . ." Olivia began with a tone that implied she didn't want to let it go.

"Not right now," I said and her face fell with a mix of sadness and annoyance. "I'm sorry . . . I just want to enjoy the day."

Olivia lifted her head and slowly nodded even though I knew it wasn't what she wanted to hear. It was still comforting to know she cared, but I wasn't ready to open up.

I had never been on a ferry before. In my head our transport for the next hour was to be a five-star liner with bottomless mimosas. Instead, it was overcrowded, with peeling paintwork and a disturbing amount of rust. We managed to find seats on the top deck and the view helped me ignore the loud snoring of the woman opposite and her wild children who found delight in using the space as a playground. I felt compelled to trip one but instead counted to ten Mississippi.

The ferry bobbed over the calm sea and I was grateful for that, knowing that my stomach was delicate when it came to sudden movements. Ruby spent the entire time reclined over three seats and regaling us with stories of the boat parties she had attended in the South of France. Tom appeared oblivious as he read a Sci-Fi novel, and Olivia pretended she couldn't hear, so it was up to me to react appropriately. I got the impression that her tales were for Olivia's benefit, and Olivia's lack of interest simply spurred Ruby on to talk more shite.

The further we got out to sea, the stronger the salty breeze became. My lioness's mane was making a show of me despite it being tied back.

"Are you cold?" Olivia asked. I protested that I was fine but she had already taken out a large beach towel and wrapped it over both our legs. She searched for my hand underneath the towel and held it there, out of view. Although the constant secrecy had become tiresome for me, the small clandestine gestures of affection were very much welcome. Ruby sat up for the first time and asked Olivia if she knew where the toilets were.

"They're just down the stairs and to the left."

"Will you show me pleeeease?" Ruby cooed in a sickly-sweet voice.

Olivia slipped her hand from mine and ushered Ruby to the lower deck.

"She's not very discreet, is she?" Tom shouted over the wind.

"What do you mean?" I asked, already knowing the answer.

"What Ruby wants, she tends to get. So just watch out when she decides to seduce Olivia! But I think Livvy has much more willpower and brain cells than I did!" Tom looked at me and we both burst out laughing.

As the ferry drew closer to the pier in Bequia I stood up and gasped at the view. The water was crystal clear; the sky was astonishingly blue and there was finally the white sand I imagined stretching for miles. It was the perfect cinematic image of a Caribbean paradise, a wish-you-were-here postcard moment complete with sun loungers, oversized umbrellas and an obligatory beach bar. I reached for my camera and took a few shots, feeling privileged I got to appreciate such beauty. There were scores of small boats parked along the shore and all I wanted was to jump off and explore the island.

"It's beautiful, isn't it?" Olivia asked from over my shoulder.

"It looks amazing!" I yelled, tripping on high expectations of sun, sea, sand and soca!

Chapter Twenty-Six

Every insecurity I had about my body suddenly seemed a huge overreaction looking at all the shapes and sizes on the beach that day. The beachwear of ninety per cent of the women should have come with complimentary blindfolds for everyone who had eyes! I thought I was a keen advocate for embracing your body, but sometimes my prissy nature would get the better of me. After the initial shock of lady lumps stretching as far as the eye could see, I began to relax and loosen my grip on my beach bag, which was covering the cellulite on my thighs. Voluptuous bodies were spilling out of ill-fitted bikinis that looked suspiciously like lingerie. Watching backsides unashamedly escape from shorts and bounce up and down to the sound system was truly hypnotising. In the far corner of the beach, under a tarpaulin marquee, were five large BBQ drums. The smells coming from them were incredible and I was more than excited to try my first bite of jerk chicken.

As we walked past the DJ, it was hard to miss the ginormous speakers stacked high on top of each other. The romping bassline of the soca music was so intense that it felt like it could have reached out and punched me straight through the heart and I would still be grinning. We settled on a stretch of sand near the action but far enough away that we were able to hear each other. Reclining onto the towel, I breathed deeply. This lifestyle was the furthest thing from my mind just a week ago, but here I was listening to great music on a tropical beach with a couple of lovely people. I guess that was one thing my father had gifted me—the opportunity to experience his beautiful home.

"Olivia, my love, be a sweetheart and help me with my suncream?" Ruby rasped.

"Um . . . okay, sure."

I rolled my eyes behind my sunglasses as Olivia smeared a gloopy layer of cream into Ruby's shoulders. After a few minutes of high-pitched giggling from Ruby, Olivia moved onto her side to face the sea. I looked up and realised I would really miss her when I left. Shit. That was never the plan. I didn't want to be one of those clichéd morons who ended up falling a little too hard for their holiday fling. It was like I was starring in a crap low-budget version of *How Stella Got Her Groove Back*. I winced at the thought of being so predictable and instantly wanted a drink.

"Do you fancy coming with me to get a drink?" I asked Olivia in a whisper so nobody else could hear.

"Absolutely!"

Although I had an annoying habit of presenting my heart to women within nanoseconds of being around them, I was keen to avoid the drama that usually entailed. I had learnt in the past that being obviously available was a huge turn-off. Playing hard to get like Noah did with his many suitors was the way to go. The only problem was I didn't play games. I didn't know how. You either liked me or you didn't. The rules of dating shouldn't have to be that difficult. The only reason I held back with offloading my mind, body and soul to Olivia was because I was far too preoccupied with my father. Usually by now I would have frightened any potential love interest with my borderline-hysterical appreciation for West End musicals. As much as I had not explicitly introduced Olivia to my interests, she had not told me anything of real substance about herself.

After making our way through the congested bar area with our drinks, I coaxed Olivia over to the other side of the beach near a giant rock formation. With our feet nestling into the edge of the waves, I felt the urge to know who the lady was behind the quirky piercings and volunteering.

"So, when you leave St Vincent in a couple of months, where to next?"

Olivia narrowed her eyes, wondering what brought on the odd question.

I laughed. "I'm just asking!"

"Well, back home to Brighton, I suppose. I have an internship at a local nature reserve." Olivia's eyes flicked with genuine excitement. It was nice to see someone who appeared to know exactly what she wanted to do in life. I nodded enthusiastically and sipped on my cocktail encased in a hollowed-out coconut shell. I hoped she wouldn't ask me my thoughts on the environment, as the conversation would have been incredibly short.

"And will you be living with your parents?" I asked, not sure if I was opening a can of worms.

"For the moment, yes, until I save enough to rent a place. My parents are both fantastic and supportive with letting me do my own thing. They give me room to breathe, be myself and experience life, but they keep me in check when I'm being obnoxious!" Olivia laughed and then suddenly stopped. "I'm sorry. Does talking about how great my parents are make you want to punch me a little?"

Now it was my time to laugh. "Not at all. Don't ever be sorry for having an awesome family."

We continued to chat and I discovered Olivia had two older brothers, her guilty pleasure was listening to Adele in the bath and she had a pet hamster called Alan. It was nice to have an idle conversation without worrying about how I was coming across. She had already seen me cry, so I could have told her anything and it still would have been less of an embarrassment. Anything. Even my unhealthy obsession with musicals.

"Why *Rent*?" She sniggered a little too hard for my liking. "Isn't it just about a bunch of overzealous people celebrating being screw-ups?"

I gasped theatrically and wedged my coconut drink into the sand as if I meant business. "Firstly, you just admitted to listening to Adele in the bath as she sings her heart out about how shit relationships are and why all her future lovers are doomed because she's clearly not over her ex! And secondly, *Rent* is about being an individual, something I know you can relate to. There's also the importance of friendships, being creative and not letting 'the man' tell you how to live your life! It's a bohemian tale of living for now. And yes, okay, being gay, drug addiction and tragically dying from AIDS-related illnesses . . . oh, and being sung back to life on a kitchen table may be part of the story. But it's all about being in the present. Well, I think it is anyways." I tailed off. I didn't realise how passionate I felt about the message of one silly little musical until that day on the beach.

"Is that why you came here? To live in the now and figure out your family stuff?"

I sighed and lifted my coconut with both hands. "I don't really know why I'm here yet. It didn't even sound like a good idea when I drunkenly booked the flights! But I'm sure I'll figure it out."

There was a silence as I looked out into the sea. Before I had a chance to exhale again, Olivia's full lips met mine, taking me by surprise as I fell onto my back. We groped each other with desperation, teasing, searching, and falling as if we were discovering the art of kissing for the very first time. It felt as if we could finally scratch a three-day-old itch of silly closeted lust. With eyes closed tightly we didn't pause, we didn't consider and we didn't care who saw our outrageous PDA. Being wrapped up with someone who enjoyed being around me as much as I did her, felt extraordinarily calming. Even if I had not yet made sense of my time on the island, I did know that Olivia allowed room for me to breathe and for my heart to beat with a new, albeit terrifying, purpose.

Walking back along the sand towards Tom and Ruby, I felt light. The music was thumping through my body like the rum. Olivia and I cut through the dance floor of sand, gyrating enthusiastically to the soca music. On any other day in any other circumstance, the dance moves performed on the beach that day would have been enough to get you arrested for indecent exposure. Women were bent over touching their toes, backing up into the groins of enthusiastic men. People were having fun. It felt primal and free. We kicked up the sand with our bare feet, stomping away to the music that was whipping us into a frenzy. It felt exuberantly free.

I collapsed next to Tom, who was tucking into some food from a paper plate. It felt odd but so satisfying to be tired from playing.

Tom grinned from ear to ear, blissfully content, fed and full. "Here, try some of this chicken. It's amazing!" He pushed the plate of chargrilled meat towards me.

I picked up the chicken leg like a caveman and bit into the soft spicy flesh. The jerk seasoning danced on my tongue, filling my whole mouth with drool. "Oh my God! This is fabulous!" I shouted, sinking my teeth into the meat again, with little regard for the mess I was making.

Tom and Olivia laughed. Ruby remained silent, her lips pursed.

"I want to dance!" Ruby abruptly declared, like an insufferable three-year-old child who wasn't getting enough attention.

"Well, okay, let's all go and dance," Olivia replied, with as much enthusiasm as she could muster.

"I'm going to sit this one out," I said. I wanted to stare at the sky, make faces out of the clouds and take more photographs. I wanted to sit in the moment for a little longer. "I'll be over to you guys in a minute."

I took out my camera and began snapping all around me. I needed to document the day and take it back home with me. Maybe when I arrived in New York I could even show my father. Perhaps I could make a photo album for him. Not only would I return his favourite toy, but I could also bring his home to life for him. I had read somewhere that in the last stages of cancer it was best to keep the patient comfortable by talking about when they were happiest. St Vincent was my father's happy place and that's what I was going to bring to him.

I suddenly felt a foreign sensation. I was getting excited at the prospect of seeing my dad. Yesterday I felt seething disdain for him, but now I wanted to make a photo collage for his viewing pleasure. Nothing was making any sense. I was still hugely apprehensive about seeing him on Friday, but it felt like the same concern I had on the plane, and St Vincent had turned out to be the best little adventure so far.

Chapter Twenty-Seven

The ferry back over to St Vincent from Bequia was much of the same, just with more noise from all the party revellers. I was still irritated by the excitable kids running around who clearly wanted to end up overboard, and Ruby was still trying her best to impress Olivia. I would have given the girl ten out of ten for effort, but the fact that Olivia spent most of the journey talking to me made me feel a little embarrassed for her. We were all tipsy at that stage, having drunk too many cocktails, and we had no intention of stopping, so it was straight to Royston's. It was my last night and I wanted to wring every last moment of pleasure from the holiday.

I couldn't recall a time when I had felt so relaxed physically or mentally, and certainly not at the same time. My shoulders no longer felt taut; I hadn't played with my shambolic hair all afternoon and my face ached from all the laughing. I had been well and truly licked with the laid-back Vincentian way of life and I didn't want to come down. It almost sounded comical how I was forced kicking and screaming to visit the island and now I didn't want to leave. Although I was feeling giddy I was determined not to get too messy, as I still had packing to do. Plus, travelling with an epic hangover sounded as much fun as cystitis when you work in retail and your lunch break is four hours away.

The sun was setting and the bar was heaving just as Royston had predicted. Tom, Olivia and I squeezed ourselves into a corner table thanks to Tom parting the sea of people and forging a path. We had lost Ruby in the battle for the bar as she finally gave up her pursuit for Olivia. I was sure I had spotted her brazenly twerking on a young gentleman ten minutes earlier. Tom sunk a bottle of beer and declared he would go and find her. I gave him a knowing look to suggest he was smitten and he said, "Oh do shut up!" and then blew me a kiss. Olivia appeared to be blankly staring out of the window. I was uncertain if I should interrupt her thoughts, so I tapped the side of my glass to the sound of the speakers and inhaled the ambiance for a little longer.

A few minutes later, I playfully slammed my empty glass onto the table in an over-the-top manner to try and get Olivia's attention. She continued to toy with remnants of a label she had ripped off a beer bottle.

"Is everything okay?" I finally asked.

"Yes, fine. I'm just done with drinking and really tired. Fancy getting out of here?"

We left the bar and wandered a few metres down the road with neither of us saying much.

"I probably should be heading back. I have to pack," I said as we came to the junction in the road.

Olivia nodded slowly.

"Okay, what's the matter?" I asked, now concerned I had said something wrong, and then the penny dropped. I straightened my back, waiting for Olivia to start the "it's not you, it's me, let's just be friends" talk.

She curved her back away from me and kicked at the ground with annoyance. "I didn't want to like you this much. I just wanted to like you a little bit. Just enough to make me smile. But now I'm mad about you and I don't want to leave things here. I don't want you to go."

"I'm . . . I'm sorry," I stuttered, clueless as to what she wanted me to say. "I'll miss you too." I reached for her shoulder trying to encourage her to turn around and look at me.

She slowly twisted her body but kept her eyes fixed on the ground, her arms crossed. I went in for a hug that lasted a few seconds longer than just good friends, and she finally relaxed into my body.

"I know this question might be very juvenile, and I'm cringing on the inside, but I just need to know. Do you really . . . urm . . . like me . . . urm . . . like that too?" Olivia asked.

"What the hell do you think?" I whispered.

She broke into a giant smile. I wasn't sure if she expected me to sweep her up like a Hollywood starlet, spin and dip her elegantly while she revealed just enough of her perfect thigh, or even tell her I loved her. But I was never going to do that because real life wasn't a 1950s movie.

We exchanged phone numbers and email addresses and I promised to call her once my phone was working again. She gave me another warm hug and slipped something into the pocket of my shorts.

"Read it when you get on the plane," she murmured into my ear. "I'm going to head back to the bar to find Tom."

Then she was gone.

I glided towards the taxi rank with fluffiness in my head and a fullness in my chest and waited for another impatient driver to take me back to the B&B. Damn I was going to miss this crazy little island. I would even miss the erratic kamikaze driving and the cursing from the driver as he blamed everyone but himself for the dangerous manoeuvring. As I entered the B&B, I heard the chatter of voices from the back. I walked towards the beautiful spicy smells of Effy's kitchen and peeked through the door. Sitting around a small table was a family of four. The father was talking to his fidgety son, who looked no older than five, "Tomorrow I will show you where I went to school," he said with excitement. His wife was waving her mobile phone in the air with frustration and shouted out to the kitchen, "Excuse me, can I have the Wi-Fi code, please?" There was a teenage daughter, too, miserably swinging her legs back and forth on a chair and staring at the empty pool.

Effy emerged from the kitchen with her usual wide grin, swinging hips and hands full of plates piled high with rice and peas and chicken. The father rubbed his hands together with delight and the teenage daughter screwed up her face.

"Maya, daaarling! You reach back already! You want sumting to eat?" Effy shouted across to me.

I shook my head. "No, no, I'm okay. I should pack. I'm leaving tomorrow. I just wanted to say thank you for having me and sharing your amazing food, if I miss you before I go."

Effy jostled over to me for a big bear hug, and wrapped her chubby arms around my waist before kissing my cheek. "Now you take care of yourself, gurl! And I hope you did find whatever it was up dere in Georgetown!"

I smiled. "Yeah, I think I did."

Ascending the steps up to my room, I saw the old man on the landing changing a light bulb. I was fully prepared for him to ignore me but he stopped and looked me up and down just like he had on the first night. "Now you lookin' much better," he said. "You look fresh! Not so pull down and vex all the time." He grinned widely and nodded, and then continued screwing in the new bulb as if nothing had been said.

I beamed, happy he had finally spoken to me, albeit slightly confused as to what he really meant. Nonetheless, I politely said thank you and then rattled open the door to my room.

I flicked on the TV and aimlessly scanned for the pirate radio station. I kicked back onto the bed and puffed out my chest. On my bedside table lay the toy car, the photograph of my mother and me and my father's letter. I looked at the photograph and for the first time in forever the ache that gripped my stomach was replaced with a faint lightness. I picked up the letter and noticed how worn the page had become. Staring at the date in the top right-hand corner, I carefully ran my fingers over the numbers 6/7/13. Twelve days had passed. It was now the eighteenth, so I still had plenty of time to see my father within the two-month window, even if he was being optimistic. I held the yellow toy car in my other hand and squeezed it tightly. I was more than ready for this. I needed this. It was time.

Chapter Twenty-Eight

It was 1969. Man walked on the moon, Woodstock showcased the legendary Janis Joplin and Jimi Hendrix, and BBC 1 and ITV broadcast in colour for the first time. The world was on the cusp of a decade of exciting innovations, new adventures and life-altering incidents. It was the year Cedric received a small yellow car for his seventh birthday, and it was also the year his mother attempted to drown him in twelve inches of bath water.

Money was always scarce and rarely spoken about among Cedric's friends and family, and toys purchased from a store were seen as unnecessary luxuries. As long as you had food on the table and a roof over your head, Georgetown was paradise. Growing up on a small island like St Vincent, the vast majority of your possessions were handmade or second-hand, and because everyone was in the same boat, Cedric never felt like he was missing out. The year before, Cedric received a red balloon and one whole fried fish and a plantain for his birthday, and he was as happy as a child who had been gifted a unicorn that burped the alphabet. However, this year his auntie from America sent over a crate of presents for the family, so for the first time Cedric would have a real toy all for himself.

With four brothers and six sisters to look after, Cedric's mother never had the opportunity to go to school and was illiterate, but she was extremely talented with her hands. If there was a gown to be sewn or a cake to be baked, she was a wizard with creating beauty from the basics. She spent most of her days weaving straw hats and elegant lace fans and then selling them either from her verandah or at her cousin's market stall in town. Cedric would often watch her masterfully weave each layer of bamboo with such precision and speed that it looked almost superhuman. Mr Thomas, Cedric's father, died before he was born and the small income his mother generated from selling the hats just about covered food and school supplies for himself and his older sister Lou Lou.

Cedric always knew there was something different about his mother, even from a young age, but what seemed strange or erratic to outsiders was his everyday normal. The locals teased and called his mum Mad Martha.

"Watch out, folks! 'Ere comes Mad Martha!'"

Cedric always thought it was a light-hearted game, as his mother would simply smile and nod at those who ridiculed her. He also knew that to question his mother would have been insubordination. On her good days, Cedric would see his mother dancing with a broom in the kitchen. Her ashen feet would sweep across the concrete floor in wild circles as she twirled like a ballerina with her skirt hitched up into her knickers and her small breasts swaying underneath her nylon vest. The elation and energy in her movements were addictive to watch and always made him laugh. Sometimes she encouraged Cedric to dance with her. On her bad days, she would lie silently in bed with the curtains closed and nothing but a glass of water on the bedside table to replenish her for the day. These days were Lou Lou's cue to take charge of the house and Cedric until Martha emerged the next morning with her signature smile and no explanation.

Cedric couldn't contain his fresh-faced ecstasy when his mother handed him the small yellow toy car over breakfast that morning. His face ached from a grin that stretched from ear to ear. Nothing could wipe the smile from his face, not even Lou Lou with her constant teasing.

"Mama! What a ting! Me carn't believe it!" Cedric flung his arms around his mother's waist, his hands struggling to connect around her wide hips. She mirrored his smile and softly stroked the back of his head.

"'Appy birt-day, son. You can play with it when you reach back from school. I'll leave it right dere." She carefully placed the toy on the kitchen table. "Now go brush ya teet before you leave, ya 'ear me?"

All day Cedric was soaring on a cloud of wonderment thinking about his birthday present. He whiled away the afternoon of maths and history with daydreaming about his toy car and the adventures he would take it on. All through the back garden, stealthily across Mr Benjamin's front porch and down to the river where he was made to wash his clothes every Saturday morning. Usually, Cedric would prolong his walk home from school by climbing coconut trees with his friends just to avoid as many chores as he could, but knowing that his most favourite thing in the world was waiting for him on the kitchen table made him hurry home in a haze of excitement.

Cedric burst into the house and raced to the kitchen but his toy car was nowhere to be seen.

"Mama? You home?" he called out, but there was no reply. His mother must have moved it which made him drop his bottom lip.

"You said it would be right dere!" Cedric called out, hoping his mother was in earshot. It was only as he sulkily stomped across the hall to his room that he heard the tap running in the bathroom. He crept closer to the bathroom door that was set ajar and peered through the gap. Cedric knew not to disturb his mother when she was in there, but when he saw his yellow car sat on the edge of the bath, he gently pushed the door and entered. Staring directly back at him was his mother, fully clothed sitting on the toilet seat. Her face was devoid of emotion but Cedric could tell she had been crying by the white dried patches of tears around her eyes and nose.

"Mama . . . you ok?"

It was as if she was staring straight through Cedric and past the gaping doorway behind him. He instantly knew something wasn't right, but he didn't want to acknowledge it. He liked to pretend the bad days weren't happening. Cedric slowly reached for his car, slipped it into his trouser pocket and forced a smile at his mother. She flashed a wide smile back. Cedric's body relaxed.

Then his mother grabbed him by the front of his school shirt and wrenched him into the bath water.

"Unclean! I must baptise you, son! You nasty . . . you need healing. God the redeemer can only heal you now!" Her speech was spikey and loud as if she was possessed by a demonic monster. She kept repeating the word "unclean" over and over again as she dunked Cedric under the water pressing down hard on his small shoulders. He thrashed around, trying to catch his breath every time her hold loosened to adjust her grip and push him under again. Cedric tried to hold onto the sides of the bath but his mother was too strong. He couldn't breathe and in that panicked moment of enduring a nightmare in real-time, Cedric hated his mother for the very first time.

Then it all went silent.

Lou Lou arrived just in time and somehow managed to haul her mother off her little brother and onto the ground. Cedric shot upright and coughed up mouthfuls of tepid limey bath water. His mother lay on the floor, curled in a ball, crying hysterically, as Lou Lou draped a towel around Cedric and hoisted him out of the bath.

"Get to your room . . . NOW!" Lou Lou shouted at Cedric.

Cedric ran as fast as he could and discarded his wet clothes on his bedroom floor. He jumped on his single bed wrapped in only a towel. He lay on his side bawling, not knowing what he had done to upset his mother. What was it about him that made him dirty and unclean, and how was he able to fix it and make his mother happy again?

Cedric spent the rest of his birthday in his room crying softly and rocking slowly back and forth. It was the first time he had gone to bed without any dinner and it was the first time he wasn't treated to his favourite dish of plantain and fried fish for his birthday.

When Lou Lou woke him for school the next morning, he momentarily forgot about the events of the day before. He rubbed the sleep out of the corner of his eyes and blinked into the sunshine coursing in through his bedroom window. He sighed peacefully, still in those first few seconds of the day where everything is slightly disorientated, the bubble between being asleep and awake, until the brain catches up and throws you rudely back into reality. Cedric's stomach suddenly sank as he recalled the previous day. He gently unclenched the palm of his hand, releasing the yellow toy car he had been squeezing the entire night.

Chapter Twenty-Nine

Yanking my suitcase from the back of the taxi made me stumble backwards into the path of a moped. The driver tooted aggressively as he swerved out of the way and I kissed my teeth. After catching my breath, I paid the driver with the last few dollars I had and didn't bother to wait for the change, as that would have been another pointless and theatrical charade. I had dressed more appropriately this time, in light colours and thin layers. I also packed a hoody in my hand luggage, as although I was told that New York would be warm in July, I didn't think it would be Caribbean hot. On the airport forecourt, I twirled around and raised my sunglasses onto my head. It was going to be a long while before I would feel the dry heat against my skin, have random men whistle at me, dance provocatively to reggae and hear passionate voices speak broken English on every corner. I could now appreciate why my father spoke so fondly of his home in the sun. St Vincent was an island of poetry, colour, exotic smells and bold characters, all set to the most infectious music. I was sure I would return someday.

The flight to Barbados felt as perilous as it had on the way over. My tray kept falling open, the seat belt wouldn't fasten properly and the plane swayed like King Kong himself was outside batting it with his fist. The only difference this time was that I knew the drill, so I had my iPod ready to drown out my gasps of fear with toe-tapping choral arrangements. The flight from

Barbados to New York was better. I had five hours to relax and attempt to watch an entire movie without falling asleep. But before that I wanted to read Olivia's note.

To the girl with the amazing hair! Just like your silly musical Rent, 'no day but today!' I'm jumping in with both feet. I don't know what you've done to me but I like it. I know that copious amounts of rum and sweaty dancing have mostly encouraged whatever we have between us, but I don't want it to end and I hope you feel the same. The unresolved upset you have going on with your dad – unfuck it! ☺ I think this will help mend your heart that you so fiercely guard. Safe travels. See you soon, and read the damn book! xx

She put two kisses at the end. That must mean she liked me.

My mind was awash with romantic feelings, alongside the nervousness of coming face to face with my father the next day. I settled into my seat and decided the best way to distract myself was with a bunch of good-looking kids killing each other in a dystopian universe. I tapped the play button on the small screen in the back of the seat in front of me and immersed myself in somebody else's drama for a change.

Five hours, an inedible lunch, two bags of peanuts and a full film later I touched down in New York. Raising the window blind, I could see bright daylight and a clear sky. It was afternoon, so I adjusted my watch to just after three o'clock and searched my bag for my passport and the address of my hotel.

Clearing immigration was a little more regimented especially as I was dressed like a hippy and my skin tone was not working in my favour. The officer behind the glass screen examined my passport a few moments longer than he had the other passengers' ahead of me. His eyes travelled from my photograph to my face and back again as he thumbed through the pages of my barely used passport.

"And where have you just come from?" He asked, despite the torn portion of the boarding pass that I left inside my passport telling him exactly where I had been.

"St Vincent via Barbados." I made sure to speak clearly and concisely so as not to provoke him into wrestling me to the ground and accusing me of smuggling drugs internally.

"Oh, I have an aunt who lives there," the officer replied with a jaunty tone as he stamped my passport and waved me onwards.

I swung my suitcase up and off the carousel and finally exiting the airport, everything seemed to be so much louder. The rattle of sound from passing vehicles and bodies coming together and splintering off in every direction made my heart beat that much faster. I waited patiently in line at the taxi rank to be ushered to a big yellow cab. I instantly felt a smile appear across my face. One of the most iconic symbols of New York City stopped next to me and the small Asian driver helped me lift my bags into the boot. I whipped out the address for the hotel and as I read it out loud he nodded enthusiastically, suggesting he knew exactly where he was going. I fell back into the pleather upholstery and breathed a deeply. My body was wrecked. Suddenly my phone began insistently beeping from inside of my bag. I finally had signal!

I had a trail of messages from Noah, starting light and breezy and then escalating to hysterical, with excessive use of the exclamation mark. "Where the hell are you?!!!!!" "Call me RIGHT NOW!!!!" So I sat back and did just that. The phone call would probably bankrupt me but I missed his voice and needed to let him know I was still alive. It would have been around nine o'clock in the evening back in London, so I knew Noah would be somewhere between the sofa and the kitchen unless he had a date.

The phone barely rang twice before it connected and Noah proceeded to scream into my ear. After the high-pitched mania and a mini monologue about why I was the best and worst friend in equal measure, how the postman had mixed up some of our post with Mo's downstairs, so we had received another final-demand bill a few weeks late. And there was a mysterious parcel for me on the kitchen table, apparently. Then he calmed down. "Now, Miss Maya Thomas, tell me everything!"

The journey from the airport to the hotel took about thirty-five minutes and I spent the whole time chatting away to Noah about my little adventure. The people, the food and my father's toy car were the main topics, followed with my brush with two intimidating men who Noah said could've "raped, murdered and pillaged me". I stared out of the window but my tired eyes couldn't focus on anything. I promised myself I would hit the tourist trail as soon as I had visited my father the next day. I was excited and intrigued by this amusement park of skyscrapers. I wanted to don an "I ♡ NY" T-shirt and take a photo with the Naked Cowboy in Times Square.

"And who is this Olivia?" Noah's voice rose with delight.

"She's just a friend!" I giggled like a schoolgirl, which even took me by surprise. "Listen, I'm just getting out of the taxi so I'll call you back once I'm checked in."

The hotel was bang in Times Square because Noah chose it and I had no real say in the matter. I apparently needed to be "among the lights and action"! Even in the daylight the visual overload of signs was painful on my retinas, but truly impressive nonetheless. There were people everywhere and it seemed quite possible to be mowed down in a hit and run by a fellow pedestrian on the pavement. The cacophony of noise, from the chatter of people passing by to car engines and horns, made me lose my breath. I sought refuge through the sliding doors of the lobby's entrance. With every step, I could hear my trainers squeaking on the pristine marble floor. The hotel was clinical compared to Effy's place. It was shinier and less homely, but I couldn't care less at that point. All I wanted was to lie in bed.

I could just see the top of the lady's head behind the check-in desk. She looked up blankly with a perfect smile that looked like it had been recycled a hundred times already that day. After giving my name, I presented my passport in exchange for a form to fill out. If Effy could have seen the formalities she would have broken out into uncontrollable laughter. And if Royston were here, he would have kissed his teeth and mumbled, "Ah, wha' di bumbaclart is dis nonsense?" I quickly scanned the form, checking I wasn't signing my life away and tiredly scribbled my name, which looked nothing like my normal signature. Just as I went to slide the form back to the lady behind the desk I saw it.

The date next to my signature was typed and read 7/19/13. The American format appeared odd to me. I hesitated for just a moment and then I slowly handed the form back to the lady. She gave me a key card to my room and pointed to the lifts down the hall, but my brain was too full of white noise to acknowledge her help. I felt sick. I ran to the lifts. I had to get to my room. I had to read the letter again.

The hallways of the hotel were like a maze. Every striped carpeted floor led to another identical corridor. My head desperately spun from left to right trying to find the correct path to my room. I checked the room number again and ran. After the third frenzied attempt at inserting my key into the door, I burst into the room and dropped my suitcase. I then frantically searched my bag to retrieve the letter. I looked at the date on the page: 6/7/13. My father had been living in America for years now. What if the date on the letter was in the American format and not the British? What if it was supposed to be 7/6/13? Had the letter been written six weeks ago and not two weeks? What if I was too late? My mouth filled with saliva and my legs buckled as I fell onto the immaculate carpeted floor. I took my phone out of the pocket of my hoody and dialled to finally listen to my voicemails from Mary. There were several over the last few days, with the last one recorded yesterday.

"Maya, you crazy girl! Answer your phone and stop being so bold! What's this about you going on holiday?"

"You better have a bloody good reason to be ignoring me, young lady!"

"Maya, you need to answer your feckin' phone! Call me as soon as you can. Sweetheart . . . it's about your dad."

The last time Mary called me sweetheart was when my mother died. My finger hovered nervously over the call button. It rang four times and then I heard Mary's voice.

Chapter Thirty

There were exactly seventy-three grey hexagons on the carpet of my hotel room. I counted them all. They looked like a Magic Eye picture from 1997. If I stared hard enough and crossed my eyes, maybe I would get sucked into a three-dimensional optical illusion. But no matter how hard I concentrated on the pattern, all I saw was generic hotel carpet.

Grieving for the loss of a father I had yet to understand felt strange. It belonged to another strain of darkness that was miles away from the reaction I had when my mother died. There were no tears, just an agonising heat of pain. As I rested my head on the side of the bed, still sitting on the floor, Mary told me how she received a phone call from my Aunt Lou Lou only yesterday. He had died on Monday, when I had just touched down in St Vincent, and his body was to be flown back to the UK. His letter must have been delayed just like our final-demand bill, and my confusion over the date left me none the wiser. Mary spoke softly and steady which unnerved me even more. She asked me if I was okay and said, "Yeah, I'm fine." He had done it to me again. He had shattered all hope of reconciliation. He had left me when I needed him and this time it was forever.

After the phone call I spent a few minutes tracing my finger over the shapes in the carpet. I then hoisted myself upwards and perched on the edge of the bed while staring mindlessly at the eggshell wall opposite me.

There was a watercolour painting of the city's skyline in a thick black frame. I don't know how long I sat there looking into nothing, but the light outside my window shifted to darkness. I was eventually bumped out of my head when my phone beeped with a text message. It was Olivia.

"Hey missy! Did u arrive ok?"

My heart lifted momentarily at her concern for my whereabouts and then fell almost immediately.

"Yes, sorry. I'm here. Thanks." I then hit the Send button. It beeped again.

"Maya, r u ok?"

"He died. I was too late. Everything was a waste of time." Send. I then turned off my phone. I stood up straight, stretched my back and then began stripping my clothes off, leaving them where they fell. I was completely naked. My body didn't feel like mine. Everything that made me who I was no longer existed. The two people who created my frizzy hair, the freckles on my face and the melanin of my skin were dead. I felt like I had no identity.

I climbed into the bath and fiddled with the gunmetal tap of the showerhead. I then sat crossed-legged in the base of the bath as the powerful stream of water washed all over me. The shock of the cold water made me feel like I couldn't breathe but I liked it that way. I rocked back and forth with my knees pulled to my chest, my eyes squeezed shut. I wanted to feel something, so I slapped myself in the face a few times. I could hear the sound of my hand against my cheeks but still felt nothing. I lashed out at other parts of my body with the open palm of my hand, but I still felt nothing.

My hands gingerly wandered up to the tops of my thighs and I trailed my index finger over my keloid scars. The raised silvered wounds served as a reminder of a darker place I hadn't revisited since I had left my hometown. Albeit a dark place, it was still my safe place. Just like climbing on top of my wardrobe as a child to abscond from the madness below, tracing a dull sewing scissor's blade across my skin offered me the solace and relief I needed, away from the confusion in my head. The pain was a strange gratifying high. It made me feel in control and alive. I pondered whether I could replicate that sensation again.

I needed to get out of the hotel room.

I hurriedly left the bathroom and burrowed through my suitcase for the closest and easiest items of clothing. Without hesitation, I dressed myself in dark jeans, a red top and a creased black blazer. I stared for a while at the king-size bed and wondered why it was necessary to have so many pillows and layers of bed linen for one person. My face was rosy and warm as I pulled my hair back off my face into a haphazard ponytail. I wanted to go out and I wanted to drink. I crammed a few essentials into a small bag—wallet, key, passport. I glanced at my phone on the bed but I didn't want to be connected to anyone that night.

As I waited for the lift, the doors flew open on my floor and an excitable young family of three spilled out. They politely said hello while struggling with their suitcases but I didn't feel like returning the greeting.

There was a different lady on the front desk, another clone of corporate hospitality. The front doors automatically opened and I stepped into mayhem. I was hit with a laser show of money exchange windows, souvenir shops and a cluster of brands stacked on top of each other demanding my attention. Instead of walking into the dense light pollution, I decided to head in the opposite direction, until the lights dimmed to hum.

I was accustomed to big-city life but New York had an overwhelming sense of expectation in the air. People had told me everyone in the Big Apple was searching for something, and I think they were right. Even the empty crisp bag that rolled past me seemed to aspire to be something more than just litter. I walked aimlessly past apartment buildings with fire escapes and shuttered shops. I turned into a residential street with buildings that looked like they had been lifted right out of the set of *Sex and the City*. I crossed over into another block that had a line of people queuing to get into a hipster-friendly jazz bar. However, it was the small illuminated window across the street that caught my eye: "$1 Pizza Slices". My stomach ached with hunger for the first time since leaving Barbados.

I carried out the giant slice of pizza on a paper plate. The cheese was hot and oily but I didn't care. I licked my fingers after the last bite mere seconds later. I knew somewhere in the back of my mind that walking around a strange city at night on my own was a terrible idea, but I felt fearless that night. I pulled my blazer closer around my body and carried on wandering through streets and crossing roads as if there was a method to my madness.

The feeling of danger made me more determined to stay out and embrace the risk. A homeless man asked me for a light and I shook my head.

"Sorry, I don't smoke."

"Useless dumb bitch!"

I laughed to myself and kept walking. On the far corner of the street there was a small rainbow flag hanging from the front of an archway. It was about time I drowned myself in the unpredictability of alcohol.

I stepped down the stairs to a faintly lit room no bigger than my flat. It reeked of sweat, cheap perfume and cigarette smoke. There was something seedy about the bar, like it was a breeding ground for dirty jokes and lustful urges. It was the type of place where you felt you could catch chlamydia just from breathing in the air. To the right, there was a small bar area and a few tables and chairs occupied mainly by men. At the front, there was a stage covered in rope lights, with a keyboard.

I headed for the bar just as the most exquisite drag queen sashayed onto the stage in platform heels as outlandish as the elaborate unicorn-inspired wig on her head. She owned the stage as if her one true vocation in life was to lip-sync the shit out of "I Will Survive". I ordered a double vodka and Coke and sat at the bar, mesmerised by the performance. I sank another double and two shots of tequila in quick succession as the drag queen's set rolled seamlessly through the repertoires of Beyoncé, ABBA, Madonna and Lady GaGa.

There was a slow round of applause from the less-than-enthused crowd. I continued to drink and my lips tingled as I downed another shot of tequila. Wiping the liquid from my bottom lip with the sleeve of my blazer, I asked the bartender to surprise me with my next drink.

"What type of drink are you looking for?"

"Something to make me forget."

He reached for a bottle tucked away under the bar and poured out a generous shot of something black into a short glass. He leaned towards me and lowered his voice. "This is something I made myself. It's called Lethe. Greek mythology says that there was a river that ran through the underworld, and when the lost souls drank from the river, it made them forget all their suffering."

He passed me the glass and waited for me to drink. I mouthed the word "Lethe" as I inspected the dark liquid swirling in the glass. It sounded like the perfect medicine to help make everything stop. I downed it in one and narrowed my eyes at the instant burn in my throat. It tasted like malt vinegar with an after kick of gravel and glass being vigorously rubbed onto my chest. The bartender laughed and smacked me on the back as I spluttered trying to find my seat again.

I blinked a few times as the corners of the room kept dimming. Music played but I had no idea what kind. The drag queen had left the stage, much to my disappointment. I had the urge to dance, but I couldn't align my senses no matter how hard I tried to use my eyes, ears and feet all at once. I attempted to make sense of the environment. An old overweight man at one of the tables was grotesquely kissing a young lad who looked no older than fifteen. He was shamelessly pawing at the child who was wearing a tight vest and white skinny jeans. Beside them were two older butch women holding hands under the table and sipping on their drinks in silence. Near the stage was a table of four young men with the obligatory straight girl who was spilling more of her cocktail than she was drinking. The corners of the room were still dipping in and out of darkness. I stood up from my stool and decided to find the toilets. I took a few steps and rubbed my eyes and that's the last thing I remember.

Chapter Thirty-One

I woke up propped against a torn armchair and blinked into a small room with a fluorescent light fixture above my head. As I shot up with fright, my head thumped and I fell backwards against the chair again.

An unfamiliar voice spoke to me: "You might want to take it a bit slower next time, sugar." If it was God, he sounded like a camp cowboy. I opened my eyes and attempted to move with less haste. I finally focused. Across the room was the drag queen, and behind her stood a large mirror with light bulbs dotted around the edge. The fact that two of the bulbs were broken tarnished the illusion of grandeur, but it still had an element of showbiz about it. She wasn't wearing her wig but rather an unflattering hair net and full makeup. She removed the hair net, and in the light, I could see she was in her fifties and had a lot less hair.

"Don't be scared. You're just having a little sit down after you fell over in spectacular fashion out there."

I remained bewildered and mute.

"Oh, where are my manners! I'm Misty Acres! You, sweetheart, can just call me Misty!" She extended her hand, which was covered in a long, sparkly, silver glove, and I shook it slowly, still dazed and confused.

Grabbing both arms of the chair, I raised myself up so I was no longer slumped. "Wh–what happened?"

"You went and got yourself shitfaced, sweetie, and fell over! So we brought you back here to chill out for a minute. Sip that glass of water and stop moving!"

I could feel my cheeks burn with embarrassment. My mouth felt dry and I could still taste the end of whatever tonic I'd thrown down my neck earlier.

"Thank you so much, and I'm so sorry. I'll get out of your way." I attempted to stand but my head wasn't having any of it.

"Sweet Lord! Just rest, woman!" Misty shouted. "There's no hurry."

She lit up a cigarette and crossed her legs, wrapping her red silk kimono around her. As she leaned back into her chair, the kimono slipped from her thigh and I couldn't help but be impressed with how silky smooth and hairless her legs were. Most days even I couldn't be arsed to shave above my kneecaps. Misty noticed me staring and smiled, almost delighted she was on display and being admired.

"So, what's got you so twisted that you figured you'd drink yourself into oblivion?" Misty breathed out a trail of smoke from the corner of her thin rouge lips.

"I'm just having a funny day. I'll be over it in the morning."

Misty tapped the end of her cigarette into an ashtray and sucked in slowly, eyeing me up and down and not believing a single word.

"Listen, honey, my life has had more twists than Oliver, so I can assure you that whatever is eating you up inside will not shock or offend me. Anyone who downs one of Bruno's shots of Lethe isn't just having a funny day. I may be a bitchy queen, but I never judge ... much."

Misty inhaled and exhaled on her cigarette as thoughts and emotions I was never able to articulate before fell freely out of me. The alcohol certainly helped. There was something about talking to a complete stranger that made it easier too. In the grand scheme of things, Misty was just a random person in a strange city who I would never see again, so I had no obligation to present my best self to her just as she had no obligation to even like me.

I told her about my mum and dad, how I was too late and how I felt I had no identity or place in the world. Misty was attentive and still except for a few nods. She lit another cigarette and pulled off her false eyelashes. The one-sided exchange lasted about thirty minutes as I concluded with "and that's why I decided to get so horribly drunk".

Misty stubbed out her cigarette and leaned into me as if she was going to tell me a juicy piece of gossip. "Do you know what I think fucks us up the most sweetie?"

"Um ... no, sorry, I don't."

"We all have this perfect fairy-tale picture in our head of how things should be. And when life veers further and further away from the ideal picture we make up in our minds, we can't handle it. We freak the hell out and create more drama to try and fix the disappointment. You had a mother who loved you so much her heart could have imploded. You had a father, RIP, who although he sounds like a complete asshole, still loved you up until he died. You have a surrogate mother who did the best she could to rear you, and you have friends who adore and support you. Bad things happen, sugar. That's just life. Hearts are broken and tears are shed, and just when you think you're getting somewhere, life can pop up and punch you in the kidneys! The pain you have right now is important, honey. How you react to it, how you transcend it and how you hide from it. Pain lets us know we're still alive. You gotta embrace the ugly side of life and still appreciate the beauty of it all."

Misty pulled her kimono tighter around her body and leaned in closer towards me. "Maya, darling, what I'm trying to say in a very long-winded fashion is this: fuck your fairy-tale, sweetheart! There's more to you than a basic happily-ever-after no matter how enticing or cosy it may sound. Your own story is not yet finished."

It was at that point I felt so inspired that I wanted to stand on a table and shout, "O Captain! My Captain!"

She was completely right. And now I wanted to change the subject.

"So what made you choose this as a profession?" I asked.

Misty howled with laughter and slapped both of her knees in delight. "I didn't choose this, sweetheart. It chose me!"

I stared at her blankly, not entirely sure how to respond.

"I was born and raised in a small Southern town where the only excitement was the annual farmers' fair or a cousin marrying another cousin! Oh, Maya darling, it was hideous existence. I conformed because I knew no better. I had a wife and two beautiful children and I taught English at the local high school. Life was the bleakest shade of vanilla you've ever seen. I slowly became strangled by my own self-made hell on earth. So, I decided to destroy everything I knew, and then I came to New York to start again." Misty looked into the mirror.

"And are you happier now?"

"I am simply me. And yes, that makes me happy. I've made some mistakes but I'm living my life with truth and honesty and I hope to do so until my dying breath. Coz, honey, when it's my time to go, I intend to leave this place like a fucking meteor!"

We sat chatting away for another hour as Misty told me how much she adored and hated New York, but she would never leave it.

"New York represents the decay of popular culture," she said. "It's so desensitised to drugs, poverty and the corruption is unbelievable, but it's my home and I would never abandon it. What about London? I've never been but would like to visit someday." Misty lit her sixth cigarette of the night.

I smiled fondly at the mention of home. "London isn't too dissimilar to New York. It's a city of excitement and multiculturalism where you can walk out of your front door and always find something to do. It allows you to fall in love and to desire to be something great. But of course like in any large city, you can feel incredibly lonely at times. That's why you need to surround yourself with good people."

There was a knock at the door, and the bartender inched his head into the dressing room. "We're closing," he barked and slammed the door.

Misty looked at her watch and gasped. "Oh gosh, sweet cheeks, it's 2 a.m. and I still need to scrape this war paint off my delicate face!"

I slowly rose from the chair, head still throbbing but at least my vision was no longer impaired. "It was so lovely talking to you, Misty. And thank you, for everything."

Misty trailed a cotton wool ball across her eyelid and then winked at me in the mirror.

"Anytime, Maya darling! Remember now, only wallow for a moment. Don't entertain it longer than you need to. We are all allowed our days of darkness, but just don't set up camp and live there."

I hesitated for a moment at her words of wisdom. Mary would have loved this Southern belle.

Misty blew me a kiss and I exhaled deeply, readying myself to attempt the journey back to my hotel.

Chapter Thirty-Two

The fresh air kicked me in the face upon leaving the bar and made me fall for the second time that evening. I quickly stood up and coolly brushed myself down as if I had completely intended to collapse. I glanced up and down the street and realised I had no idea as in which direction I should walk. I instinctively went to look for my phone and then remembered I had left it in the hotel. The hotel I couldn't remember the name of. I knew it was somewhere near Times Square, but aside from that unhelpful piece of information, I was stuck. I searched through my pockets, patting myself down until I found the key card for my room. The hotel name was printed on the front. Result. I stumbled a few metres towards voices and streetlights and hailed the first cab I saw.

The night porter of the hotel tipped his top hat as I entered the lobby but his face was full of judgement as I tripped ever so slightly on my own foot. My head was still throbbing and my movements were conspicuously slow and cautious. After meandering up and down the corridors several times, I finally managed to find my room. At the fourth attempt at trying to align the key card with the slot in the handle, I kicked the door in frustration and then yelped in pain. A stern-looking old Asian lady, poked her head out from her room two doors down to investigate. I waved and smiled weakly; she glared and slammed her door.

Once in my room, I pushed the surplus pillows onto the floor and fell onto the bed fully clothed. I gazed up at the ceiling. I knew that drinking on my own was a bad idea but the whole point of that evening was to deviate from the script. I would deal with the hangover tomorrow but all I wanted was to wallow a little longer. I fetched the crumpled letter from my father and held it close to my chest with both hands and began to cry. I stayed in that position until the morning.

The only time I left my bed for the following two days was to use the toilet and answer the door to room service. I showered once and then climbed back into bed with the curtains closed. I had no energy for anything else. I ate very little and slept for hours. I was fully aware I was missing out on exploring New York City but I just didn't care. It felt as if there was a toy monkey inside my brain continuously bashing its cymbals together, and the only way to drown out the din was to sleep. I kept my phone off and thought very little of how worried Mary, Noah or Olivia might be. I needed and wanted to be completely selfish.

I woke up some time late on Monday morning and stumbled to the bathroom, still refusing to turn on any lights or open the curtains. I got back into bed but I couldn't force myself to fall asleep again. The clock on the bedside table read 11:50 a.m., and across the room my bag was still where I had left it upon arrival. I needed to distract myself, so I retrieved Olivia's book from my backpack and began to read. If anything was going to distract my mind from the present, it was the philosophising of someone who must have experimented with drugs. By the time I glanced over at the clock two and a half hours later, I was already three-quarters of the way through the paperback.

Some of the chapters were eye-roll inducing, but there was nothing outrageous about the book. As I thumbed through each page, I felt myself being drawn into an alternative way of thinking that somehow was making a lot of sense. It was all based on the practice of gratitude and the importance of saying thank you for all you have instead of focusing on what we don't have. We receive what we give out was the basic concept. To a certain extent that is what I was doing and it was exhausting. Misty said to wallow for just a moment, but I had been cocooned in my self-loathing for three days now, and it didn't take a PhD to determine how unhealthy that was. If I was putting out misery, there was no surprise I was going to receive more misery into my life. My heart still ached over my father, not just with grief at losing him, but with disappointment and regret. Lying alone in a hotel room wasn't going to ease the anguish, though. It was time to cross over to the other side.

As soon as I turned my phone back on it erupted with missed-call notifications and text messages from Noah, Mary and Olivia. Reading through the frightened messages, I felt like a bit of bitch. There were people in my life who genuinely cared about me and I had made them panic. They didn't deserve that. I started with Mary. The ringtone ran into her voicemail. She would have been five hours ahead of me and on a Monday night, meant she was down her local social club having her weekly gossip and gin. I left a message explaining how sorry I was for going AWOL, that all will be fine and I would be home on Wednesday. Next was Noah. I sent him a text to let him know I was still alive and that under no circumstances, especially not "just because he was bored", could he open my parcel, despite how interesting it looked. And finally, Olivia. She was only an hour ahead of New York time and so I had the urge to call her.

She picked up instantly and after a few excitable greetings, her voice became serious. "So, next time you wanna scare the shit out of me, please don't turn your phone off. I was imagining all sorts and I was about twenty minutes away from begging, borrowing and stealing enough to book a flight to New York, hunt you down and then kick your ass!"

Her dramatics made me think that she and Noah would get on just fine. I laughed out loud. It was nice to have someone feel so passionately about my well-being after knowing me for just a week. It was as if I was starring in my own cheesy rom-com, but I didn't care because it felt good.

"So I read your book!" I piped up, trying to change the subject.

"And? What did you think?"

"Well for the first time in three days I feel an overwhelming need to get out of my pyjamas and open the curtains!"

I could almost hear Olivia smile down the phone.

After chatting about drag queens, lethal liquor, Tom and Ruby hooking up again and Royston still being aloof but oh-so-handsome, I promised I would keep my phone on and call when I got back home. Upon opening my curtains and unlocking the window a less-than-generous but health-and-safety-compliant forty-five-degrees, I noticed the view for the very first time. The iconic New York skyline that hung on my wall was staring back at me. Just below were hundreds of people scurrying around, all absorbed in their own little bubbles. I wanted to be among them. I wanted to eat a hot dog, watch a street performer and then feel awkward when they asked for money, and I wanted to buy tacky useless souvenirs like an apron that doubled up as a bottle opener and a frisbee.

It felt refreshing to be dressed in something other than my tear-stained pyjamas complete with crusty BBQ sauce stains from the chips I had ordered to my room two nights ago. Dressed in a loose T-shirt and jeans, I slung my backpack over my shoulders and headed out. As I stepped out onto the street, I shielded my eyes and reached for my sunglasses. Being out in natural light again made my eyes water but I felt a small burst of exhilaration in my chest.

I was starving, so I headed for a hot dog cart next door to the hotel. There were always hot dog carts dotted throughout central London late on a Friday or Saturday night, but unlike the food vendors on the mean streets of London, the NYC hot dogs filled me with confidence that I wasn't going to end up with food poisoning. I had yet to figure out the exchange rate, so I was probably being financially ruined for the sake of a sausage, some onions and lashings of ketchup, but ruination was certainly delicious.

I continued to walk through crowds of people and over zebra crossings, all the while praying I wouldn't get run over by a yellow taxi. Every possible fast food chain cluttered the streets, and giant advertising boards for the latest movies sat alongside hoardings for luxury consumer goods. *A Rolex watch, you say? A snip at just $1 million!* As I continued walking, gawking like a child at the circus, I found that I had wandered into a procession of Hare Krishna monks. Dressed in bright-orange robes and scarves, with flowers around their necks, a group of ten bald-headed men sang to the accompaniment of drums, tambourines and an accordion. Their faces were filled with so much joy and jubilation that it was infectious. I felt rooted to the spot, dazzled and somewhat embarrassed at the impromptu dance routine. Nevertheless, their lack of vanity and pure enjoyment for what they were doing made it all seem perfectly normal. My body relaxed. I clapped to the beat of the drum with a goofy smile, and revelled in the moment.

As the monks moved on, I turned to walk away with a slight skip. I spent the next hour drifting contently through shops and taking photographs of the weird and wonderful. I strolled through Central Park as if I belonged there, despite my New York baseball cap and incessant photograph-taking. The world around me still felt artificial and fragile, as if I would be snatched from the daydream at any moment and expelled, returning to reality. But I needed to ignore the pangs of real life just for today.

After chomping on a Cronut, a pastry that can't decide if it's a doughnut or croissant, I left the enormous park and walked back to Times Square. Amid the neon signs there were digital billboards for famous Broadway shows like *The Phantom of the Opera*, *The Lion King* and *Wicked*. In between the bright lights and two women dressed in stars-and-stripes bikinis, I spotted something that made my heart jump. It was smaller than the giant eye-grabbing electronic adverts but it was certainly there: "Rent: No Day but Today".

It was a poster for an off-Broadway revival of *Rent* stuck to the side of a ticket booth. New York may have just won my heart.

Chapter Thirty-Three

When my mother and I went to see *Fame* in the West End, she told me I had to make an effort with my outfit. I hated dressing up unnecessarily, especially for something where we effectively would be sitting in darkness for a couple of hours. But I was so elated that I could get tickets to see *Rent* on my last night in New York that I dressed as if I was taking myself on a date. I looked in the mirror at the wildness of my hair and considered disciplining the curls, but reluctantly gave up. I had decided for just one evening I would try being me in all my imperfect glory. Even if that meant the unpredictable hair breaking for the border, or a squashy stomach rolling over the top of my trousers.

The small theatre was only a short taxi ride from my hotel, the sort of taxi ride that was entirely unnecessary, as I could have walked if I wasn't too lazy to look at a bloody map. I was super anxious not to be late, so naturally I was the first person to arrive. The usher at the door handed me a programme and pointed to the bar area where I could sit down and wait. As I sat on an appallingly upholstered cushioned stool, I absentmindedly ran my hand across the underside of the table I was perched at. I then shuddered in disgust as I fingered the fossilised chewing gum left by past theatre-goers.

The bar began filling up with more and more people. Couples, groups of friends and a few conservative-looking folks who I'm sure were not prepared for the storyline. Looking at all the faces, I began to feel terribly homesick. The sinking feeling of being alone resurfaced. I started to play with my hair and tug at my top, which was beginning to feel too snug around the middle. The excitement of wandering across the world on a solo expedition was losing its sparkle. My mission was null and void now and I was just a girl on her own in a big city. I threw the remains of my wine down my throat to try to suppress the lonely feeling. Suddenly there was an announcement over the Tannoy system, inviting us all to take our seats, and I was grateful to have my thoughts interrupted.

I had paid extra for a great seat after past experiences made me realise that frugality with theatre seats effectively led to watching a performance of ants. Sometimes I landed so far away from the stage, that I might as well have just waited until it came out on DVD. As I attempted to relax into my plush velvet chair I thought of Mary and how jealous she would have been. It was 8 p.m. exactly when the first bars of the piano intro belted out.

"Five hundred twenty-five thousand six hundred minutes . . . how do you measure, measure a year?"

As the actors took their final bow I clapped so hard that my hands were stinging. The small theatre was shaking with rapturous applause and whistles, and I ached with nostalgic happiness as though I were treating my fifteen-year-old self. I felt inspired with a sense of possibility and control over my own life and the direction it was going. Even if that feeling was fleeting, and even if I was caught up in the electricity of an off-Broadway show, I wanted to bathe in the possibility that I could conquer the chaos in my head and create something worthwhile and beautiful. The musical may have been a feel-good fantasy, but even so, if a heroin addict could be sung back to life by a cast of impossibly good-looking individuals, maybe there was hope for me yet.

I exited the theatre onto the footpath and decided I was going to walk back to my hotel. It would be the last time I would get to see the city at night and I wanted to montage through the last hours with a goofy smile and complete disregard for what brought me to New York in the first place. As I walked, I made sure to look up so I could appreciate not only the action right in front of me but also the kaleidoscopic of colour above. After a few minutes of walking, I was pulled towards the sounds coming from a doorway slightly obscured from the street. There was no signage to suggest what was inside. Even though it looked like the entrance to the final level of 8-bit arcade game *Streets of Rage*, the sweet sound of Althea and Donna's reggae hit "Uptown Top Ranking" made me trust it.

I peered into the window beside the doorway but the dirty glass made it hard to see what was inside. With a quick glance over my shoulder, I descended the few steps into the room towards the speakers that were calling me in. Inside was a small disorganised record shop with boxes of vinyl propped up against walls and doors. The walls without crates of records leaning against them were decorated with hundreds of posters overlapping each other. Janis Joplin, Jimmy Hendrix and a full-length cardboard cut-out of Michael Jackson stood near the cash register. A customer in his early twenties stood with oversized headphones plugged into a turntable. He was wearing the tightest corduroy trousers I had ever seen and I prayed he wouldn't turn towards me for fear that the outline of his manhood would be too obvious to avoid.

It was like Aladdin's cave of retro music. I excitedly ran my fingers over a film of dust that lay on top of the shelved section labelled M–N. The grime and disarray of the shop made me love it even more. It was the epitome of a hipster goldmine but without trying too hard to be a "cool shithole". So many places in London had transformed into try-hard establishments with vintage furniture and bespoke upcycled décor just so they could charge ludicrous prices. This record shop wasn't trying to be retro and cool, it simply was. I yanked a copy of Bob Marley's *Exodus* album from the shelf and saw a $5 sticker on it. I spun the LP around to the track listing on the back and a musty scent flew up my nose. It smelt of my childhood and the culture I was only now beginning to appreciate.

We are all reared on the music of our parents. Those are the rules. Until you are old enough to form an opinion on what music you love and hate, your parent's favourite bands are your main influences. Growing up in predominantly white suburban England, this could have been The Beatles, Elvis or The Rolling Stones, cut with a chorus or two from Cliff Richard's "Congratulations". But for me mainstream popular music on the radio and

TV often felt like a diluted compound compared to my father's reggae collection.

Black music was all I knew. It was rebellious and unapologetically so. Although the arrangement of a Broadway musical made me feel inexplicably hopeful and light, the music that reverberated from my father's portable stereo when I was a child made me feel powerful. It also forced me to embrace and confront the black part of my heritage. I had never really explored the black within my white until St Vincent, just as I had never acknowledged the Scottish in my West Indian. Black music made me tap into the other part of my soul. My trip across the Atlantic was slowly making me realise that soca, calypso and reggae were sewn into the fabric of my father's DNA and this in turn was part of my identity, however much I had tried to distance myself from who he was.

"I'll be with you just in a minute!" A female voice came from somewhere behind the stacked boxes near the front of the shop and knocked me out of my reverie. I smiled and walked to the till with the record under my arm.

Chapter Thirty-Four

I sauntered back to my hotel with my $5 purchase of Mr Marley. I wanted to marinate a little longer in the fresh flavours of NYC. I stopped to buy a sweet crepe from a small lady who complimented me on my accent.

"Oh, you British! You sound so freakin' adorable! I just can't deal!"

She gave me an extra dollop of syrup and chocolate sprinkles, because the double cream alone wasn't enough to clog up my arteries. I ambled slowly through the streets, content with my gluttony and smiling at the bright lights. There was a sense of magic that the city has just when you need it. If I looked past the bewildering pace and noise, I saw why native New Yorkers would never choose to live anywhere else. The porter at the hotel tipped his hat as usual, but this time there was no judgement or concerned looks as I skipped across the glossy lobby floor and into the lift.

I emptied the contents of my bag onto the bed, ready to pack. The yellow toy car fell and rolled across the carpeted floor until it stalled at a pile of clothes. I looked at it for a while with mild disgust, contemplating whether I should stomp it under foot and erase the memory of ever having found it. But I reluctantly retrieved it and tossed it into my backpack. I wanted to believe my trip had some genuine purpose. I couldn't help feeling like my efforts were a giant waste of time. It was my father who had inspired the trip. He was the lynchpin, and without him nothing made sense. In his letter he had said he loved me, but words were easy and could be used and abused, especially when you're at your most desperate. I wanted to look him in the eyes and ask him if he had ever truly loved me.

My father's death dashed any hope of closure. There wasn't a moment of relief and I couldn't map my feelings or understand how I was going to heal from it all. But maybe some things never truly healed. Perhaps life really wasn't all rainbows, lollipops and following the Yellow Brick Road to the Emerald City. Perhaps I just had to learn to adapt to the pain and embrace the occasional emotional meltdown while shopping in the aisles of a supermarket on an idle Tuesday. Grief was an emotion born from the love of the person you had lost, but in that moment, I was finding it difficult to feel love, when all I had was resentment. I was lamenting my what-ifs. What if I had contacted him years ago? What if I had just forgiven him? What if I had stopped blaming myself? I knew then that I would have to live with never having been able to say goodbye. I just wanted to tap the heels of my shoes three times and get the hell home.

Watching the planes on the runway, I thought about how this would be my final long-haul flight for a while. Thank the baby Jesus! My phone vibrated in my pocket and distracted me from my staring contest with the rear end of a Boeing 747. It was a text from Olivia: "I hope the flight home is ok. R u sad that your lil adventure is over? x"

I looked up for a moment, trying to decide if I was indeed sad, but my emotions were still all over the place.

Even though I felt ready to go home I would miss the freedom of waking up each day with no routine or plans. Soon enough I would be back at work, cursing Mo and his boxes at the bottom of the stairs and trying to manage my floundering finances.

"Sad, yes . . . I think. A little. I don't know! And thank you . . . I will let you know when I'm back in Blighty!" I missed Olivia. But I planned to tell Noah about her with an air of indifference, when in reality I was infatuated.

The loudspeaker called my flight number and I shuffled to the gate, trying my best to ignore my fellow passengers, most of whom believed there was a race to board the plane first. We were all moving in the same direction and we all had allocated seating, but still some people treated queuing like it was gladiatorial combat. There was no use in anger. I was spent on all negative sentiments and simply wanted to relax on my journey home. I was happy to have a window seat away from the family of six and their screaming kids who had no concept of the word "share" when it came to their mother's iPad. A young gentleman with a beard to rival Noah's sat down next to me. We exchanged polite smiles, and fidgeted for a while, trying to get comfortable as much as our economy seats would allow. My bearded companion began foraging around in his satchel until he finally pulled out a familiar book, *M for Metanoia*. I looked out of the window and smiled.

Dragging an oversized bag onto the Tube in rush hour was another badly thought-out plan of mine. I felt like I hadn't washed in weeks and my mouth still tasted of the aeroplane meal, more like feet than chicken arrabiata. At least I just had to sit still for the next thirty minutes before I had to change lines. I slipped my headphones on and people-watched to the soundtrack of every number-one song from 1998.

A middle-aged man in his late fifties sits opposite me. He is called Arthur. Dressed in a navy pinstripe suit, a crisp white shirt and a black tie. He is reading the Times and is on his way to the office after a strained breakfast with his wife. He knows he should end his affair with his mistress but feels that he's in too deep. He's very handsome for an older guy, with his designer stubble, so I can see the appeal. There is a brown leather briefcase on his lap and inside is a packed lunch. Pinned to the top of the lunchbox is a note from his wife wishing him a happy twenty-fifth wedding anniversary.

Standing to the left of me is yummy mummy Caroline. Her face is flushed and her hair is greasy. She's wearing designer active wear and carries a rolled-up yoga mat under her arm. She's clutching a coffee cup in one hand and her smartphone in the other as she carefully deletes last night's drunken text messages to the intern at work. Caroline hasn't updated her social media profiles in a while because she's been too busy visiting her sick mum in hospital. She adjusts her footing and tries to discreetly pull her Lycra leggings away from being consumed by her prominent camel toe.

And then there's Maya. Sitting perfectly still except for her right hand, which is tapping the outside of her knee to the bassline of another cheesy pop song. The relentless rubbing of her temples suggests she is irritable or exhausted or both.

Just as I tried to think up another elaborate detail to my story, the train halted at Green Park and Caroline moved to exit the carriage. As she walked towards the door she briefly glanced down at me with a knowing look and I wearily smiled back. The doors began to beep. "Please mind the gap."

Chapter Thirty-Five

I was away for just ten days but it felt like so much longer than that. Although I hadn't got the closure I was hoping for, something inside me had changed. But as I exited the Tube station and walked back to my flat, London was the same as ever. The popcorn still smelt the same, the lavender joss sticks still burned, the friendly Romanian man was still smiling, and the Jamaicans still bopped around to their reggae with rolled tobacco and marijuana dangling from their lips. The protest from the other week was forgotten. People had other battles to fight.

As I fiddled with my key in the lock of the door, Mo tapped on the window from inside of the chicken shop and scared the crap out of me. I waved back but I didn't want to stop for a chat so continued struggling to get my suitcase over the threshold. There were a few letters on the shelf, which mostly looked like bills mixed with correspondence from our local MP to "the occupants", no doubt about how great the plans to rejuvenate the area were. I gathered them up with my one free hand and headed up the stairs.

Noah was at work but had left me a note under a magnet on the fridge door: "Welcome home, beautiful! Can't wait to see you! Look inside . . . tonight we dine like gods!" I opened the fridge door to find a pizza and a bottle of Monk. There was also a weird-looking cheese poorly wrapped in cling film that made me gag at the smell. I certainly was home.

I flicked on the kettle and looked forward to my first decent cuppa in what felt like forever. As the kettle boiled I texted Olivia to let her know I was back. I was a little worried I was already becoming too desperate, so I deleted one of the kisses at the end of the message. One kiss was still friendly enough and suggested flirtatious undertones, whereas two kisses could be perceived as "Please love me and let's adopt a cat together. Immediately. Thanks." The kettle wheezed and startled me. I lost all concentration and buggered up the text completely. I ended up sending three kisses. *Shit.*

Half-covered with takeaway menus on top of the microwave sat the parcel Noah had been banging on about. I picked up the bulky package and examined the label. It was from America and addressed to me, but I didn't recognise the handwriting. I pulled up a chair at the kitchen table and sipped my perfect cup of tea while trying to rip into the parcel with my other hand. A small note fell out during my tussle with the brown paper.

Dear Maya,

Please find enclosed the only possessions your father had with him at his time of death in the hospice. We are so sorry for your loss. Cedric was one of our favourite patients here. He was always laughing and often spoke about you and his beloved St Vincent. We hope these items bring you a sense of comfort at this sad time.

Kind regards,

All the nurses from the Mary Seacole Hospice.

My heart began pounding. I felt nauseous and my tea now tasted like murky rainwater. I reached into the parcel and pulled out a small shoebox. Carefully lifting the lid, I could already feel my eyes welling up. Bundled among lots of tissue paper and bubble wrap were two framed photographs. There was a sepia picture of my mother and father on their wedding day and a second photo of all three of us when I was a baby. My hands shook while I cradled both photographs as if I had been searching for them my whole life. I continued to rummage inside the box and my face lit up when I found something I hadn't seen for years: my mother's plastic beaker with "I Love Scotland" written across the front. I laughed out loud. Out of everything my father could have kept, he chose to keep my mother's favourite cup.

My old man was far from perfect. His flaws were ghastly and terrifying. He abandoned me when I needed him and then died before either one of us could repair our relationship. But despite it all, he was still my father and he was still my unsung hero. I thought I needed to know if he ever really loved my mother and me and I longed to hear him say he was sorry. But as I held the plastic beaker in my hands, I could see his heart belonged to us right until the end.

I spoke to Mary on the phone and after she regaled me with stories of her bingo win and some fella called Derek being far too forward at the social club, she told me how the funeral for my father was to take place the next day.

"He's going to be buried at a church near where your aunt lives, in Kent. Do you think you will make it?"

I thought for a moment but decided I wasn't ready to be among practical strangers mourning my father in public. Whether that made me a terrible daughter, I wasn't sure, but I would be the one left dealing with my heartbreak at the end of the day, so I had to look after myself. I made a promise that once the initial shock and upset had subsided and got back to normal, I would have my own memorial for my father. I unzipped my backpack and took out the yellow car. I no longer had feelings of contempt for it. I carefully packed up the photographs, the plastic cup and the car into the shoebox and closed the lid.

Noah was overjoyed with his giant foam finger and NYC hoody I had bought for him. I missed his hugs and the way he made me feel giddy, even when I was wiped out from jetlag and sad memories. We briefly spoke about my father but I wasn't prepared for the pity just yet, so I changed the subject.

Noah had shaved his ginger beard because he wanted to try a different look for his new dating profile.

"Are you at least going to give the guy a second date?" I asked, with a mouthful of pizza.

"Well, I've provisionally said yes . . . so we will see!" Noah replied, with a cheeky glint in his eye.

"Just so you know, I am unbelievably grateful for the money you loaned me and I will pay it back as soon as possible. I promise!" Although it would take me many months to even make a dent in the amount, and even though I had already said this to Noah at least six times that evening, I needed him to know I wouldn't forget what he had done for me.

My phone beeped. It was Olivia. She hadn't replied for hours so I had already come to accept the fact she now hated me. The three kisses at the end of the text message clearly pushed her over the edge.

"Glad u made it home in 1 piece! I already miss u xxx"

My face broke out into a huge smile.

"Who's that?" Noah asked, with one eyebrow raised.

"Oh, just that girl I was telling you about before. Nothing too exciting. But she put three kisses at the end of her text so I think she's a bit keen!"

I sat back into the sofa contentedly swigging on my wine and overthinking the next text I would send Olivia. Life wasn't perfect but like Misty said, there was more to me than just a simple happily-ever-after. My story was still unfinished.

Chapter Thirty-Six

It was 2013. Same-sex marriage was passed in the UK, 3D printers were creating prosthetic ears for patients, and the Pope, who looked suspiciously like a Sith Lord from *Star Wars,* resigned. London was unexpectedly bathed in sunshine for two whole weeks. Opinions were instantly split between those who enjoyed complaining about the weather being too hot or "close", and the more optimistic ones who embraced the tropical glitch in the matrix and relished wearing crocheted bikini tops for dress-down Friday at work. I hovered in the middle. On one hand, I wanted to peel off my skin in the claustrophobic oven known as the London Underground, and on other I longed to stay perfectly catatonic in a beer garden for the foreseeable future.

I decided to throw myself back into my old routine of work and socialising the moment I had returned from New York. I knew that if I kept myself busy I could find a way to file away my thoughts. It was in this state of half-living that made stumbling unaware into an armed robbery so easy.

I took a deep breath and pushed the door of the off-licence. The shimmer of the wind chime signalled I was indeed ready and willing to destroy my liver yet again with another bottle of judgemental Monk wine. I had already prepared myself for the awkward exchange with the pissed-off lady on the till, so I readied my game face as if I was heading into a war. I selected the bottle from the shelf and approached the front of the shop. There was a tall man next to the counter wearing an oversized coat and talking to the lady on the till. I remembered thinking that London was in the middle of a heatwave, so why on earth was he wearing a giant anorak? Something felt wrong. The shop lady was visibly uncomfortable and kept glancing over at me. I stepped forward and her eyes suddenly widened as if she was trying to tell me something. I stopped moving and she slowly shook her head. I then quickly glanced over my shoulder in case she wasn't trying to get my attention at all, but I was the only other person in the shop. I knew something was out of place and I should have just left, but I continued walking towards her and the strange man in the coat.

As I placed the bottle of wine on the counter I attempted to discreetly peek to the right of the crisp stand at the lunatic in the parka. While pretending to be interested in a packet of pork scratchings, I recognised him. It was the same young man who had his girlfriend pinned to a wall by her throat a few weeks ago outside Mo's, and who I grappled to the ground like a deranged WWE wrestler. He was very skinny and topless underneath, with dirty baggy jeans and equally filthy trainers that may have been white in a previous life. He was gnawing at the inside of his mouth and tapping his hand impatiently at the side of his leg. He rotated his body to face me I spotted the small gun inside his coat.

I didn't know if he recognised my face or if he just panicked, knowing I had seen his gun.

"This doesn't concern you, lady!" he barked at me and wiped the sweat from his forehead.

I should have run and called for help but I couldn't leave the woman on her own.

"You should leave—now!" He snapped, but still I remained silent and immobile. Safety in numbers. The lady behind the till was now stood with her back up against the rows of cigarettes, trying to stay as far away as possible from the young lad and his weapon. Her eyes were glistening with tears and I didn't have a plan.

"I said move yourself or you will get some of this!" He revealed the gun and extended his arm. The barrel was facing directly at me. The woman behind the till screamed and ducked. I threw my hands in the air and swallowed hard. There was a gun pointing in my face, and although my heart was manically attempting to smash its way out of my chest, I welcomed the danger. The thrill of death made the blood in my head pump hard and loud. I stayed perfectly still and watched the right hand of the young man shake uncontrollably while his left hand wiped the sweat from his forehead again.

It felt like an extraterrestrial being had taken over my body and was using me as a host while it handled the threatening situation. I could sense my limbs moving, but it was as if I was watching myself on TV, cowering behind a cushion and screaming "Run, fool!" at the counterfeit version of myself who was now standing toe to toe with one man and his gun. I lowered my arms slowly and cautiously, aware that any swift movements would only scare him more. I didn't want to make him do something stupid. I reached out towards the gun and decided to out-stupid him. I walked towards the gun and gently moved his hand and the muzzle onto the middle of my chest. I held the gun tightly against the front of my white blouse and exhaled.

"If you want to kill me, then please do hurry up and get it over with." I could feel a tear roll down my cheek and onto my chin, but I remained still.

The young man raised his eyebrows, his finger shaking on the trigger. He looked at the woman crouching behind the till as if he needed confirmation of what I had just said.

"You are one fucked-up lady, do you know that?"

He lowered the gun.

"Yes. I already know. But thanks." I replied, a punch of cockiness in my voice.

We continued to stare at each other in a twisted blinking contest. His eyes were bloodshot and his pupils dilated. I counted in my head. One Mississippi, two Mississippi, three Mississippi. I reached seven Mississippi and he abruptly let out a crazed hysterical laugh.

"This isn't even worth it!" He tucked the gun into his grimy jeans and ran out of the door.

I turned to the lady behind the till and she carefully rose from the ground with a stricken look of disbelief across her face.

"So, what was the plan there?" She asked aggressively.

"There was no plan." I picked up the bottle of Monk without paying and left the shop.

The blast of adrenaline subsided after I closed the front door of my flat and burst into tears. It wasn't just the fact I was threatened at gunpoint that made me vomit twice into the kitchen sink, it was the fact I was willing to die. No, it was far more terrifying than that. I was genuinely excited about the prospect of dying and buzzing off the thought of a bullet shooting into my chest. I just wanted the idiot in the anorak to pull the trigger and end me. I wiped the remainder of the sick from the corner of my mouth with the back of my hand, and frantically unscrewed the lid of the bottle of wine. I chugged on the sharp acidic liquid until I needed to take another breath.

My entire body felt like someone had scrunched me up like a sheet of grease-stained fish-and-chips paper and tossed me towards the bin. The only problem was that they missed and I was laying useless and soiled on the floor. My clothes and my skin felt scratchy, tight and constricting. I tore at my blouse in a frenzy until the buttons popped off and flew in various directions across the kitchen table. My thighs felt like they were on fire, so I roughly pulled my trousers down to my ankles. Standing in my open shirt with my underwear on display, I breathed heavily. I needed air. I needed a release. On the draining board near the sink, a corkscrew lay on its side and I reached for the smooth wooden handle. I slowly slumped down onto the kitchen floor and placed the sharp metallic point on the top of my exposed thigh. One Mississippi, two Mississippi, three Mississippi. With one deep breath, I trailed the tip of the corkscrew across my skin and I didn't breathe out until the bloody line was drawn.

Chapter Thirty-Seven

Two weeks passed and the normality I was expecting to resume never materialised. I began to think that the events of the past few weeks were like swallowing chewing gum and would take seven years to digest. I found myself retreating further into my thoughts and dancing with dangerous ideas swilling around in my head. Familiar but toxic ideas about how to permanently stop the panic came back to me like an old friend. Yet I still smiled through the day, entertained Noah's latest dating conquest and engaged in banter with the Rastas outside of the Tube station.

"I'm going to visit my aunt tomorrow," I texted Olivia late one evening.

She didn't reply until I had arrived at Victoria station on Saturday morning.

"I think that's a gr8 idea . . . let me know wat happens x"

The concourse of any large railway station always disorients me. It's the hordes of people of all shapes and colours making their way through inert crowds to get across the country. Everyone is on a quest to be somewhere faster than the rest, and the selfish nature of big-city life means that our own journey is far more important than anyone else's.

I was holding an almond croissant purchased from a French patisserie, which oozed as much romantic charm as every other food stall dotted around the station. I looked up at the electronic boards for my platform number and calculated I had twelve minutes before departure. As I chomped on my croissant I absentmindedly watched a gammy-legged pigeon hobbling across the ground with a chip in its mouth. Although it looked like it was in desperate need of first aid, it still looked as menacing as if it was packing a switchblade underneath his mangled feathers.

Mary had given me the address of my Auntie Lou Lou's place and the name of the church where my father was buried. I didn't bother ringing ahead as I was secretly hoping my aunt would be out so I could avoid the uncomfortable conversation of two related strangers with nothing in common but a dead man.

The train carriage was half empty so I easily found a window seat. Watching the world go by from a train window was as therapeutic as listening to a medley of show tunes. The train gently crept away from the station and I listened to my iPod, observing the landscape shift from industrial to suburban to countryside. I was an hour and a half away from the seaside town of Margate, so it was a perfect interlude in which to smother my anxiety with the entire score of *Wicked*.

An hour and a half, one weak cup of tea and a packet of cheese and onion crisps later, I was pushing through a crowd of people in the ticket hall at Margate train station. It was lunchtime and as I left the arches of the train station I shielded my eyes from the brightness of the sun. There were lots of families milling around holding balloons and oversized cuddly toys. There was an amusement park nearby, so it all made sense as I watched a small child bawl her eyes out after her ice cream fell to the ground. I reached into my jeans pocket for the piece of paper with my aunt's address on. I wasn't in the mood for aimlessly walking around—I just wanted to get this part of my trip out of the way. I crossed the road and hailed the nearest taxi. I presented the address to the driver. He nodded and then moved off.

Seven minutes later we pulled into a small street lined with grand, identical, red brick townhouses. The roofs were flat and there were at least three storeys to each building, with a basement.

"Here you go, love!" the taxi driver said above the noise of an advert for a furniture sale on the radio.

I handed him the fare and slowly got out of the car. I nervously adjusted my backpack and suddenly felt ridiculous for not ringing ahead. Like, who even does that? Just show up on the doorstep of a practical stranger. *Great plan, Maya, you giant idiot.*

I stood staring at the stone steps that were covered in different shades of damp moss. I sheepishly ascended the steps to the door and held my breath until I reached the top. My hand reached for the brass knocker as I banged three times and stepped back.

"Please be out. Please be out," I muttered under my breath.

There didn't appear to be any movement within. No sound or curious twitching from net curtains. I breathed a sigh of relief and backed away from the front door.

"Excuse me, can I help you?" A voice travelled from over my shoulder.

I swivelled on the spot and found myself staring at a lean black woman with tight braids pulled back from her face. She was holding what looked like hundreds of shopping bags. Her defined biceps flexed in her short-sleeved top. She carefully rested the bags on the ground and lifted her large tortoiseshell sunglasses onto the top of her head. I forgot how much she looked like my father.

"Maya? Good Lord, is that you, girl?"

I nodded as if I was terrified it would fall from my shoulders. I then did something neither one of us were prepared for. I ran down the steps and hugged her as if I hadn't embraced another human being since forever.

Once we got inside the house, Auntie Lou Lou handed me a glass of lemonade with a red and white striped straw. Her house was like a page ripped from the home and lifestyle supplements Mary would get with her Sunday papers. Crisp, clean edges, carefully considered throws draped over expensive-looking sofas, a country-style kitchen with an Aga and a Belfast sink. My aunt packed away her shopping and I perched awkwardly on a stool. The walls were covered with family portraits of people I assumed were my cousins. Graduation photographs, weddings and babies.

"You should have told me you were coming. I would have made more of an effort," Auntie Lou Lou said as she passed me a tin of homemade muffins. Her accent was very soft and terribly middle-class. I couldn't detect a hint of West Indian, not like my father, which was surprising since she was older than him. I briefly

229

wondered what it was that allowed England to strip her accent.

"Those are my children and grandchildren." She motioned towards the wall.

I noticed a certificate from King's College London that read "Louisa Thomas, LLB Law".

She saw me looking at it and explained, "I have my own practice now but I tend to work from home."

I was unsure whose benefit that was for, but I smiled nonetheless.

"I'm sorry I missed his funeral." I didn't know why I said that. I wasn't sorry at all but I felt compelled to apologise out of politeness and steer the chat back to the reason for my visit.

My aunt lowered her head. "Yes, well he had a good send-off. It was small, but nice. It would have been even nicer if you had been there."

She looked at me with a hint of judgement which made me instantly straighten my back and cross my arms. How dare she! How dare she stand in front of me with her posh accent flaunting her perfect family, toned biceps and expensive home in my orphaned face! If only she knew the reasons behind my reluctance to celebrate the life of my father. Maybe I should have told her exactly the type of man her precious brother was. I was getting angry and stood up from the stool. But quickly realised I was only angry at myself. Although I wasn't ready to be at his funeral so soon after returning from my trip, there was a strange sense of guilt for not being there. I calmed my thoughts, pushed a stray frazzled curl behind my ear and sat back down on the chair.

"Do you have any photographs of him?" I asked.

Chapter Thirty-Eight

I carefully thumbed through a small burgundy photo album no bigger than an A5 notebook. The cellophane sheets were dog-eared and the once-white backing had a yellow hue that matched the photographs. Aunt Lou Lou stood over my shoulder and narrated each picture.

"That's your dad in his Sunday best, ready for church . . . That was a neighbour's birthday party . . . That there was Mr Benjamin who lived next door . . . And that was your grandma. She unfortunately suffered from bipolar disorder, but back then everyone just dismissed her as being crazy. If only she had the medical treatment sooner . . ." Aunt Lou Lou trailed off and I pretended I couldn't see her wipe away a tear.

I looked intently at the older woman in the frame. She was very slim and wasn't smiling. She was standing rigid, wearing an apron and thick black glasses. I had never seen a photo of any of my grandparents before. It was oddly comforting to know I had a real family tree and to see what she actually looked like compared to the Tom and Jerry-styled mammy character I had imagined for years.

"And that was the day before we all left for England. Your dad is carrying his toy car. He would never let it out of his sight! He loved that thing." My aunt chuckled.

There in plain sight was the yellow toy car I had dug out of the ground. The smile stretched across my father's little face was beautiful. I wanted to tell my aunt of my adventure in St Vincent, but I wasn't ready for the barrage of questions that would surely follow, so I said nothing.

"Things changed once we arrived here. Gone were the lightness and merriment of our days in St Vincent. It wasn't only the weather that was cold here, but the people too. At first your father still had a cheery disposition. Cracking jokes and finding the humour in life. Even when Mama was placed in a care home he still kept both of our spirits up. He also had a marvellous resilience to prejudice, something I wish I had. He was happy to keep plodding on despite the ignorance we faced, whereas I needed to prove myself. I wanted to blend in, Cedric not so much. Our phone calls and visits became less frequent after . . . your mother's death." My aunt sighed and rubbed her temples.

"Cedric could have been so much more. I wish he was so much more."

I remained silent, unsure what to say, as I too believed my father could've done something far more amazing with his life. I thought about telling my aunt how his resilience and cheerful outlook did finally snap, but nothing would have been gained from that. I passed the album back to her.

"No, no, I think you should keep it. I have copies and the memories, but I think you should have this. Maya, I know you were estranged from your father and I don't understand the circumstances or particularly wish to know, but I do know this: Cedric loved you more than life itself." She smiled and wiped another tear from her face.

I noisily inhaled the last dregs of the lemonade after demolishing my second muffin and looked at my phone for the time. The two hours with my aunt surprisingly had flown by as we spoke about her grown-up kids and her "brilliantly intelligent" husband who was an engineer and away with work. She was very good at extracting information out of me without me noticing, like my job, whom I lived with and my marital status. But I was very aware that although we were related, we were not close. I chose not to disclose details of my relationship or where I saw myself in five years' time. I needed to be on the 16.42 train back to London, so it was time to leave for the cemetery.

"Thank you for having me, Auntie Lou Lou," I said, heading towards the front door.

"Oh, good gosh! Nobody has called me Lou Lou since, well, since your father."

We looked at each other and smiled.

"Maya, let me know when you get home and don't be a stranger now! You are family, after all."

I waved to her from the bottom of the steps and felt a warm feeling of satisfaction. My aunt was the only link left to my dad and a family I knew very little about. I wanted to keep the connection alive. The Baptist church was a twenty-minute walk away, so I squinted down the road into the sunshine and set off at a purposeful pace.

The road in front of the church was jammed full of cars. According to the ageing caretaker pottering around at the front gates, it was a perfect spot to park for the weekend because it was free.

"This is the house of God, not a convenient car park for joy seekers and amusement park enthusiasts!" he told me.

"Um, is it okay if I head to the graveyard?" I asked quietly, in case I upset him further. He looked right through me, eyeballing a family of four reversing into a space and then answered, "Yes, yes, around the back to the left."

I walked cautiously behind the main church building and came across a handwritten sign that read "Please keep off the grass", which I read in the voice of the angry caretaker. The first plot of land was no bigger than a London back garden. There were about twenty headstones and I found myself heading for the back row, which had a fresh mound of gravel and bouquets of flowers. As I drew nearer to the spot my heart fluttered and my mouth filled with saliva. I crouched down and read the brass plaque on the front of a temporary wooden cross.

CEDRIC THOMAS, RIP

1964–2013

I wasn't sure what I was expecting but it wasn't that. In my head, I believed I would be screaming into the air "Whhhyyyy!" and tearing into the soil with my bare hands in some vain dramatic attempt to find the closure I was looking for. I wanted to stop the anxiety that had been sitting on my chest ever since I read his letter. But most of all I wanted to know why my mother made us stay with him. Why did she put us both through hell for all those years? All I felt was a rush of love for a man I once knew. It was infuriating, but finally pennies began to drop, everywhere.

My mother never left because she loved him. That much was obvious and it was something I had always considered to be a weakness. No matter how much she wanted to hate him she simply couldn't, and I could never understand why. But as I idly traced the edges of the small wooden cross with my index finger, I felt it for the first time. No matter how much I wanted to hate him, I simply couldn't. All this time I thought it was the regret of not hearing my father apologise and say how much he loved me that hurt the most, but I think it was the missed opportunity of me telling him I still loved him that broke me.

But I didn't think I could forgive him. It probably would have been easier, and perhaps the lack of forgiveness tarnished my love, but there was still a dark pain inside me that wouldn't allow me to tidy my emotions away for the sake of a picture-perfect ending. Forgiveness takes time. Staring at his grave, it was clear to me now. My trip to St Vincent and New York proved our bond was inescapable. But I would be damned to ever allow myself to condone or accept his violence. Despite the love and the memories that consumed me, I felt like I would never gift my father forgiveness. Love and forgiveness are two separate things.

I didn't cry. I thought I would but I didn't, even though ugly crying in public places is something I excel at. I also didn't feel like destroying an inanimate object in a fit of rage. Instead, I sat cross-legged at the base of my father's grave and simply whispered, "Hi, Dad, it's me." I took out my phone, scrolled through my library of music and pressed play on the playlist I had created the night before. It was filled with old reggae songs that reminded me of him and the moments of my childhood I still adored. I stretched my body across the grass and lay on my back with my hands clasped behind my head. I stared up into the clouds and watched a flock of birds chasing each other in formation. I then closed my eyes and let the lyrics of every song form a conversation between my father and me.

Thirty-five minutes later I opened my eyes to loud coughing from behind me. I bolted up, startled. "Crap! Sorry!" I blurted out to the disapproving face of the caretaker. "I think I just drifted off for a moment."

"Yes, well, I'm sorry to interrupt you but I'm closing the gates for the afternoon. The opening hours are printed clearly on the gate."

I rolled my eyes and kissed my teeth, before gathering up my bag and phone. I lingered for a few seconds longer and looked back at what was left of my father.

"Night, night, Dad. Sleep tight and don't let dem blasted bed bugs bite."

Chapter Thirty-Nine

It began with my hands. They felt sweaty but I put that down to the lack of cool air on the Tube during rush hour. I felt like I had just left a Latvian sauna after being violently beaten with leafy branches. It was now the uncomfortable pulsating in my chest and hands that made me stop in aisle two at the supermarket, between the pasta and rice and the ethnic food section. My hands involuntarily twitched despite me trying to Jedi-mind-trick my nervous system into controlling the convulsions. I shook my hands, hoping it would either confuse them or stop the twitching altogether. It didn't do either. I decided my next tack was denial. I ignored the panic and continued towards the chilled food aisle to select the perfect microwave-ready lasagne for dinner. I lifted the pre-packaged block of lasagne from the fridge and flipped over the box, pretending I knew what I was looking at. It was good to know they were marketing it as an authentic Italian meal even though I could have been purchasing minced baby Ostrich and be none the wiser.

As the lasagne hit the bottom of my shopping basket, the sensation in my hands and chest travelled to the pit of my stomach. I choked on a wave of nausea and suddenly realised I was unable to breathe. I felt hot and my head was awash with background noise. I doubled over and dropped my basket and bag. My heart felt as if it was going to carve its way out of my chest with a blunt instrument. I closed my eyes and counted with tears streaming down my face. I had reached sixty-two Mississippis when I felt a hand on my shoulder. I sprung up and saw the concerned eyes of an old lady mouthing words to me I couldn't correctly decipher in my head.

"Are—you—OK—dear?" the old lady asked but still I was confused.

I shamefully collected the contents of my bag, which had spilled across the shiny tiled floor. I threw my tin of Vaseline and the last stray tampon into my bag and ran out the sliding shop doors into the street.

That was the third time in a week. I felt like I was losing control. At first I blamed jetlag, then I blamed my menstrual cycle until finally I blamed the emotional hangover from my father's death and the visit to his grave. There was still a problem, despite my visit to Kent last weekend, but I wasn't sure how or if I could fix it.

I knew deep down that to work through my issues and save the princess at the end of the game, I had to battle through perilous levels of dungeons, dragons and immovable objects. I knew I had to grapple my way out of my comfort zone, but one problem remained: I only had a Zone 1–2 Travelcard and I wasn't prepared to travel any farther than that. I needed a force majeure to make me realise how messed up my life really was.

Later that evening, I sat down on the sofa and poured my second glass of Monk. Recently I had taken to self-medicating with cheap wine followed by inhaling lines of crushed codeine tablets bought from two separate chemists. Noah was at a performance poetry night in Covent Garden. He had invited me, but the thought of clicking my fingers by way of applause for a poem about love disguised as war but really about the political and social structure of working-class London was not how I wanted to spend my Thursday night. All I wanted was to be left alone. I took another gulp of my wine and continued to stare at the cracks snaking their way up the wall behind the stereo. My eyes felt heavy but I was determined to drink through it. I crushed another tablet on top of the coffee table with a teaspoon and snorted.

I woke up to the morning sun leaking through the living-room curtains and the sight of an empty bottle of Monk on its side. It was 7.03 a.m. I must've fallen asleep on the sofa. The disgust and disappointment was immediate. My mouth tasted of wine and fried onion from one of Mo's burgers. I hoisted myself into an upright position and burst into tears.

* * *

I decided to grab a coffee instead of my usual chai latte. It wasn't a ground-breaking change to my routine but I was all about baby steps. Work had been insanely busy since I returned. I guess that's what happens when you up and leave last-minute-dot-com. Although I had been back for six weeks, there was still a never-ending trail of paperwork stacked up on my desk pleading with me to file, shred or respond to it in some way, shape or form. At least it distracted me from 9 a.m. until 5.30 p.m. each day. My colleagues initially tiptoed around me, unsure as to whether they could ask about my father and his health. I told my boss he had died, and by lunchtime that day, there was a sympathy card and flowers lying across the keyboard of my computer.

That day, however, I had been clock-watching since midday. I scrolled through Facebook and clicked enviously through Olivia's latest photographs. She would be back in the UK in a few weeks and we had already planned for me to venture down to Brighton. The days of overthinking my texts, wondering if things were moving too fast and acting nonchalant to Noah about my true feelings for her were long gone. I still liked her and she still liked me. For what reason, I had no idea, but I decided to roll with it. If anything, knowing I would get to hang out with her again had made the previous few weeks somewhat bearable. But who knew? I might discover that once the glow of travel and holiday adventures had worn off, and the newness of "us" had expired, that we were just two people who once had something in common. But for the time being, I wanted to embrace the terrifying experiment of living for the moment.

I hadn't felt comfortable in my outfit all day. For some reason my white blouse and black trousers that were my go-to work attire were pissing me off. As I ordered my coffee, I fidgeted with the hem of my blouse. The barista shouted out "Sharon!" impatiently holding up a cup of what appeared to be my coffee. I waited for a moment in case there was a Sharon who would claim it, but of course no. Apparently "Maya" sounded like "Sharon". Apparently the barista was a complete moron. Noah would have been horrified at the lack of personality in the coffee shop. Although he could have earned a lot more if he worked for these "corporate wankers". Noah loved his independent café family more than the extra £3 an hour he would get if he sold out.

* * *

I took out the crinkled piece of paper from my purse and checked the street name again. I had never been that far west on the Tube line before, but the write-up on the website assured me it was highly reputable. The terraced houses looked like the Chelsea Flower Show had puked up all over them. It was a stark contrast to my road with its empty polystyrene chip boxes on the paths and overgrown front gardens occupied by abandoned sofas. Part of me wanted to find an excuse, turn around and postpone this meeting. The other part of me just wanted it over with.

I finally stopped at a large Edwardian house. I looked at the piece of paper again and then back at the building. I neared the stained-glass door and realised it was the correct address when I read the name of the practice on the doorbell. There was a crackle through the intercom as I nervously announced my name. The latch clicked open. I breathed deeply and hesitantly crossed the threshold.

The last few weeks leading up to this meeting I had been the worst possible version of myself. I had unintentionally lost weight, replaced meals with alcohol and cried myself to sleep. One night I even frightened Noah by returning home sporting a bloodied gash above my left eye after a late-night drinking session with work. I was so intoxicated that I had no recollection of how it happened. I spent weeknights drinking heavily and the weekends hiding under my duvet. Noah would try to coax me out of my room, inviting me to comedy gigs, shopping trips or just to watch another one of his subtitled arthouse DVDs. But I felt depleted. There were things in my head I still needed to release but I didn't know how.

It all came to a head one evening when I was taking a shower. I hadn't eaten much that day and felt lightheaded for what felt like just a few seconds. I eventually woke up wedged between the miniature bath and the toilet seat, wrestling with the broken shower curtain. Noah came bursting through the door and for the first time saw the self-inflicted scars on my thighs. He hesitated for a moment then quickly wrapped me in a towel. I proceeded to sob for an hour, leaning against Noah and the radiator. It was clear to both of us that I needed to speak to someone. It was finally time to unfuck myself.

"So, Maya, what brings you here and what would you like to talk about?"

I took a deep breath and counted in my head. "One Mississippi, two Mississippi, three Mississippi, four Mississippi, five Mississippi." I unclenched my right fist. I was squeezing so hard that I had left a red imprint on the palm of my hand and tiny half-moon indentations from where my nails had dug into my skin. I carefully placed my father's yellow toy car on the small table next to me.

"Well, it all kind of started with this."

Acknowledgments

There have been so many movers and shakers who have helped me write this story which started back in 2015. Whether it was those who I personally know or random burps of inspiration from people watching on a bus ride into town.

Big love to: Jenny Price, who entertained me banging on about a possible-sort of-story-thing I had in my head while we sat in a coffee shop in Norway. Phil Jackson, who read my very first draft in full, and despite it resembling something a 3-year-old had written with crayons, he still told me I was a hoot and a 10! And Dee Shine, who helped me craft subplots when my brain melted, listened to me moan, and always talked me down from a ledge when I was being overly dramatic.

Big thanks to: Mary Stanley, who offered me those initial kind words of encouragement when I had zero clue what I was doing. Vanessa O'Loughlin, who kept telling me "more colour!" and pushed me to dig deep with my writing voice. Robert Doran (ninja editor extraordinaire) who really gets my rambling words whilst carving out something truly wonderful. And Design for Writers, who once again made an awesome cover design.

Big hugs to: Sami, Kristin and Allayne, who read and critiqued the opening chapters to help me decide if I should continue… or just give up as a writer and drink more vodka.

And big slowmo high fives to: everyone who took the time to read this book. Being a storyteller doesn't really work if you don't have anyone to tell your story to. So, thank you… you're lovely and have a great smile!

13625528R00148

Printed in Germany
by Amazon Distribution
GmbH, Leipzig